The Beautiful Abyss

Gini Chin

ACKNOWLEDGMENTS

I owe a great deal of thanks to my ever-patient writing group.
I could not have done this without you.
You stuck by my side for years.
Also a huge thank you to David Poulshock for his endless
support and words of encouragement.

The Beautiful Abyss

PROLOGUE

*He who fights with monsters might take care
lest he thereby become a monster.*

— Friedrich Nietzsche

1993 Istanbul

At a waterside table, I peeled the giant steamed prawns, sucked the meat out of their heads, and dipped crisp, puffy *yufka* bread into their juices. Champagne tickled my throat and cut through the prawn's buttery liquor.

I paid the bill for my dinner and headed back to the Pasha Yali, a private eighteenth-century villa on the Bosphorus. The streets and alleys were still crowded with tourists. Music tumbled out of every shop and bar but faded as I left the district. Water lapped at the edge of the villa. I climbed the grand staircase to the master bedroom with hope for a fresh start to Thof's and my relationship. I was looking for the reset button to the chaos and bad decisions we had both made in the last year.

"Just in time! There's one glass of champagne left. It's a good one," Thof proclaimed, bringing me a glass.

His usual pristine shirt was untucked and wrinkled. I studied him as he made his way across the room. I could have sworn he stumbled on the edge of the rug. He was sweating, even though there was a light breeze, and his eyes were glistening.

"You are the most gorgeous woman in the world."

"You're not so bad yourself, Thof."

He put his arms around me and pulled me in tight.

"I feel like I could break you in two like a little bird." He grinned and pressed his lips hard against mine. His piercing blue eyes were the color of the sky on a clear, sunny day. I arched backwards against his weight. "Come feel it with me," he said.

"Ow! That hurts. Feel what?"

"I want to show you the full transformation tonight. It's time. The fox has arrived. And so, too, will your other lover. Very soon, I'm sure. I just got off the phone with him."

"What? What are you talking about?" I was so confused. How could he have known about Costa? Anyway, Costa and I had ended it. This weekend was supposed to be a fresh start for Thof and me.

"Are you okay? What about your meeting?" I brushed over his comment.

"I'm better than I can ever remember. And what about your meetings? I know all about you and Costa. You are quite the liar, aren't you? But no worries, my little kit; there'll be no need for that anymore." He looked away from me and sniffed the air like a dog. "My gawd, it's hot."

"Maybe you should sit down. Tell me about your dinner. Mine was fantastic." I pretended to ignore what he'd said about Costa. What the hell did he mean that Costa would arrive soon?

Thof paced around the opulent room. His strange, twitchy behavior was making me nervous. I needed something to fiddle with and picked a lemon out of a large crystal bowl mounded with the yellow orbs and studied it.

He ripped his clothes off, ignoring what I'd said, and even more, what I *hadn't* said. The buttons popped off his shirt and skated across the floor, disappearing into the lush hair of the white yak rug. He turned to the satin-sheeted bed, whose leather headboard was trimmed with gilded baroque flourishes. It was nearly as big as a pool, and he did a running jump into it like a boy doing a back flop into the deep end. I followed him, desperate to get information out of him about his dinner with Brielle. I'd agreed to this trip. Agreed to trust him to have dinner (and nothing else) with Brielle. Agreed to restart our relationship. I missed his raw cravings for me, the way his body fit mine perfectly, like notches on a puzzle piece. Costa had been a mere distraction compared to Thof, who had taught me to embrace my beauty and power and run with the moon.

But now I wanted some answers.

He pulled me down on top of him.

"You're drenched in sweat," I complained.

"Because you're so hot." He flipped me over onto my stomach, then pulled my dress up and my underwear aside, grabbing me around my waist and pulling me up on all fours. "Just like a dog," he snarled.

"Stop! Are you on something?" I raised up on my knees, arching backwards like I learned to do ten years earlier in a self-defense class. "What the hell are you doing?"

Thrown off balance in a half stupor, half rage, he fell off me, onto the floor.

"Help me, Niki," he shuddered, his back heaving up and down as he gulped air, whining.

My instinct was to reach out to him, but I hesitated, and in a flash, he was on me again. When I reached up to block him, he grabbed my wrist and yanked me from the bed. My head slammed the floor and stopped me cold. Reflexively, I curled up and was seized with a blinding headache. He came at me from behind and rammed himself into me, hammering me against the cold marble. Spit flew from his mouth and his sweat rained down on me. He yanked my hair, all the while whooping and giggling like a hyena. He finished fast and was off me, pacing the room as though looking for an escape route.

I watched him clench and unclench his fists with no self-consciousness of his nakedness as he rifled around in his pants pockets looking for something. Then he popped something in his mouth, balled up the pants, and swigged the last bit of champagne from the bottle. "This is good pharm. Better than anything," he said.

Wiping his mouth on his arm, he stood bare-assed and

twitching on the balcony, then came back into the room and stood over my curled-up body. I held my head moaning, threw up on the floor and rolled away from it. Couldn't he see the pain I was in? Couldn't he smell it?

"*Niki, get up*! Are you listening to me?" He kicked me as I lay on my side. The ball of his foot landed squarely on a rib, and I heard a distinct snapping sound. I screamed, but stopped short as the pain shot through my back like a searing iron. "You've got to try this shit," he said as he rifled through his pants again. He pulled out another pill and handed it to me, but then swallowed the pill himself.

"Where the fuck is the champagne?" He picked up the phone and screamed into it at whoever was on the other end to bring a bottle to the room, then headed out to the balcony again. His yelling had been loud enough that passersby below looked up to see a naked, hairy man hunched over the railing of a balcony just a few feet above their heads. They quickly scattered as his body streamed sweat and spittle flew from his mouth. Then the howling started.

I'd slowly been making my way across the floor, dragging myself toward the door, hoping he wouldn't notice. His tirade washed over me in waves as I floated in and out of consciousness from the pain. I couldn't analyze or reason anything. All I could do was try to get away. But my body moved as though through quicksand. Like in a nightmare.

"Niiikkkkiiii!" he yelled toward the water as if I was a Siren miles away instead of an injured woman just a few feet inside the room.

The depth of emotion in his voice was like a child being ripped away from its mother. I recognized his fear and the vast emptiness, but Jesus, I must have lost my mind thinking this was going to work. I broke down crying as the pounding on the other side of the door started.

"Open the door, Mr. Fiomako. We're coming in." Keys jangled in the lock, then the door swung open straight into my back. I spewed blood and threw up again. They rushed the room as if expecting to find more than just the two of us. Only Baris, the concierge, kneeled down to check on me.

"Mr. Fiomako, step away from the balcony!" a policeman yelled.

"I'm going to rip her throat out!" Thof screamed. The crowd below gasped in unison.

"Get a robe," a policeman ordered Baris as they cuffed Thof and strong-armed him back into the room. "And a medic for the woman."

PART I

1

1988 Oregon

It was the middle of the afternoon, and I decided to quit work early and get some fresh air. I was a freelance graphic designer, with no boss other than myself, so I could do whatever the hell I chose to do. I walked home, across the railroad tracks and up the hill to our house at the end of a dead-end street in the woods. A breeze had finally gotten around to blowing the stagnant air out of the valley, which had the town on a smog alert. An agricultural haze from tilling dry earth and burning grass, along with a low-pressure system between the mountains and the ocean, had kept the scratchy air on lockdown for days.

Jin's chocolate brown Fiat convertible, his baby, was parked in front of the house. He was obsessed with two things in life: cars and his body. Odd, I thought; he would normally have driven it to work.

In college, we'd driven that car many times, top down, through the night, from Eugene to San Francisco on quests for dim sum that reminded him of home, and for trendy new clothing for me. We bundled up in our winter coats for the eight-hour drive, the freezing wind keeping us awake, daring ourselves to keep the top down all the way. Eventually the heater melted into a hard blob of molten plastic and had to be replaced.

I climbed the stairs up from the street to the house, which was perched on the side of a steep hill. "Bad feng shui!" my mother-in-law had informed me years ago about its street address. The numbers added up to four. In Chinese, the number four sounds very similar in pronunciation to the word *death*.

I heard giggling when I opened the front door and called out to Jin, "What's so funny up there?"

"Hello?" I called up to the loft again. No answer. I kicked off my shoes and went upstairs. The phone cord stretched from the bedside table to under the sheets, where Jin writhed, panting and moaning. I stood silent and motionless for a beat, not wanting to believe what I thought I was seeing.

"Hello?" I said louder this time.

Jin's head popped out from under the covers, face flushed.

"What are you doing?" I asked him. He was still under the covers as he slammed the phone down. "It was a wrong number, Niki," Jin answered in an angry tone. "I was trying to nap because I don't feel good. What's your problem?"

"I heard you laughing." I could feel my face turning red. Why was he mad at me? What had I done?

Jin scowled. "I'm sick of your tone. You're always nagging; your lips are pursed. Stop it. It's not flattering."

My eyes welled up. I'd been self-conscious about my looks since I was twelve when my friends and even family teased me. Bucky Bucky Beaver, they called me. "You can't close your mouth, can you? You gonna catch some flies?" my brother and sister taunted. "Close your mouth; I can hear you breathing!" my mother complained. My mouth was literally too small for all my teeth, which buckled in on themselves like train cars gone off the track. Eight teeth were pulled and bands were hammered on. Wires fed through the bands were tightened monthly. The pain was so bad I'd throw up. Two and a half years later a picture-perfect smile was unveiled. In spite of it, when I saw my reflection in windows or the unexpected department store mirror, I cringed and quickly looked away, still ashamed of my profile.

I left Jin under his covers and quietly retreated to the kitchen to make dinner. I shut up and shut down.

While the pasta boiled, I noticed the pile of mail on the dining table and shuffled through it. Bills, bills, bills. Jin had never allowed me to handle them, even after five years of marriage. He said he didn't trust me to do them correctly or keep them organized. I'd conceded. But now, I thought, fuck it. Fuck him. I randomly chose the phone bill.

I tore it open.

My life changed.

I discovered the reason for our sexless marriage and his insistence that I not touch the mail: phone numbers with the 900 area code filled page after page. The bill was hundreds of dollars. Phone sex.

The fucking bastard.

. . .

The very next day I called a travel agent. I didn't tell Jin I was leaving until my tickets arrived. I couldn't risk letting him change my mind. That gaudy yellow necklace his mother gave me on our wedding day finally came off my neck and would pay my way to Europe. I waited until the day before I left to sell it, as he would have noticed if I wasn't wearing it. If he asked me about it, I'd lie and tell him I was leaving it at home for safekeeping, that I didn't want it drawing attention and risk it being stolen.

Hocking the chain at a pawn shop downtown made me feel like a thief, though, as if I'd stolen it from his mother. I justified selling it by reminding myself it had been a gift. But it was fraught with emotions, expectations, and complicated ties. Handing it over to the gruff man behind the counter, feeling the weight of it slip out of my hand, brought tears to my eyes. Our marriage could be summed up with a transaction in a store with bars on the windows.

I thought about where it had come from. I'd been to his home town in Malaysia where hawkers enticed you with samples and treats to enter their tiny stores in the open-air markets. Theirs was "number one!"—gold, fabric, precious stones, antique pottery. All shiny and glimmering. What was Jin's mother thinking when she bought it for me?

...

Jin was the first born, therefore the most precious, and his marriage the most important. He was expected to be the most successful, most reliable, most prosperous. The chosen one. So why had he chosen me? I wasn't in his league by any stretch of the imagination, not by intelligence, family status, or economic position, and especially not in refinement.

Why hadn't he chosen any of the handfuls of silken-skinned, rich, highly educated girls from upper-class families like his own where he grew up, or from the many expats on campus? The only possible answer was citizenship. They all wanted it. I was his ticket. So unknowingly, I traded him nationality for gold. He and his fellow Malays wanted out of their country with its stifling government and impossible cultural and familial expectations. They whispered about it as though they were still being surveilled. They'd done their required two years of military service before they left for college so they would be free to *not* return. Ever. How could I have been so naive not to see it? His attraction to me was a business transaction. My attraction to him was exotic infatuation.

2

A month in Europe sounded like a well-deserved break and enough time to decide what I wanted. It was about time I got some perspective on our relationship, and more importantly, why I alone felt the responsibility for its success. Jin was gone when the taxi came to take me to the airport. We picked up Pema, my best friend and sister-in-law (we were married to brothers), who I begged to come with me, and off we went.

…

Pema and I had met Jin and his younger brother, Bing, in college and the four of us had become best friends. Before Jin, my only long-term relationship had been with my high school sweetheart, who I cheated on during the four years we were together and eventually jilted for Jin, who was older, strikingly tall, and more exotic than anyone I'd ever known. He'd swept me off my feet, but the minute the ring went on my finger the sex stopped. He told me I smelled funny "down there," laughed at the sexy lingerie I tried on for him, and giggled nervously when I tried to touch him. It made me feel like I'd done something perverted. I couldn't put my finger on why that giggle made me feel so dirty, and it crossed my mind that maybe he was gay. Maybe he pursued and married me as a cover from being outed.

Off to counseling we went, but sex was somehow never brought up. It was as though Jin had bribed the therapists. We'd seen many over the years. I even conceded to seeing a man, thinking Jin would be more open. In the end, we learned how to communicate better—don't interrupt, be respectful—so we could fight quietly. The relationship survived on vapors.

I'd stayed with him for all the other benefits—money, travel, a beautiful house, new cars, trophy husband—all of which I didn't believe I deserved. I was brought up to believe I'd be a hard-working, middle-class wife who bought instant potatoes in a box and had a factory job, like my mother had. Jin was my escape from all that.

But five years later and thousands of dollars spent on counseling, we still had a sexless marriage. Madonna-whore complex, my own counselor told me. Men want to marry a virgin and have sex with a whore. It ended up only he was having sex with himself, so I guess he was the whore.

I told myself to smile and be perfect. I knew no other way. I actually didn't know how to be happy or pleasant, for him or me or anyone. I hadn't learned a thing in all that time. My only hope was to fake it. But it never lasted more than a minute. I'd been attempting it since I was five years old, trying to placate my mother, who was a narcissist and cheated on my father. I was emotionally alone—as a child and as a wife. I was young and had more possessions than anyone needed, which made me feel guilty for still being unhappy. It was a vicious cycle. I felt selfish for wanting more, for wanting emotional intimacy, for wanting to be seen, for wanting to be heard.

...

After weeks of traveling in the sweltering Mediterranean summer heat, we were low on money and very much on each other's nerves. We'd been through Bruges, Salzburg, Siena, the Cinque Terre, and more. The last leg of our trip was Greece. We flipped a coin and picked one last town off the beaten path before heading to Santorini, where Pema had spent some time during college and wanted to revisit.

At three in the morning, we shoved and elbowed our way through the crowd as we were herded like cattle off the ferry from Brindisi to Athens and found the bus for Nafplio. This town had better be a doozy, I thought. Last chance! I dozed off while Pema started up a conversation with a fellow passenger.

"Chuck," he introduced himself to her, was headed to Nafplio, too. He looked like a Muppet in a faded blue Hawaiian shirt that was two sizes too big for him, white painter pants, and round, frameless glasses that were too small for his dark sun-creased face. A paint-splotched baseball cap caged the wild, scraggly hair ballooning out from under it.

He was taking the bus back to town after leaving his motorcycle to be fixed in Athens, then was going to a party for the night. He had a Southern accent that came and went as he talked. He insisted we have drinks with his friend the next evening. Oh gawd, I thought, eyes closed, pretending not to listen, What has Pema gotten us into now? Chuck talked incessantly about American politics, alligators (he was from Florida), and his sailboat.

Shaken to pieces by the cranky bus, we finally got to Nafplio. Walking through the cobblestone streets to the square, we dumped our backpacks on yet another bench and collapsed.

"Now what? Why do we always arrive in new towns before dawn? I can't go on like this. I've never been so exhausted or hungry in my life." I couldn't stop complaining. "Can we please book a room before we leave for Santorini?" I asked, but Pema was already nodding off.

Clattering shutters and banging chairs woke us from our drowse as shopkeepers set up with the rising sun. Used to the sight of ragged tourists, a cafe owner asked us if we needed a room, and the request went out from grocer to baker to tchotchke shop owner, down the line, like they'd done since

Jesus' time, until in a matter of minutes we were following a scowling old woman up an old staircase.

"*Diavatírio*," she said as she extended the palm of her hand. Pema and I looked at each other blankly. "*Passaporta!*" she huffed.

We handed them over, like we'd done so many times, at the mercy of a stranger. She slammed them shut in a drawer, locking it with a loud jangle from a ring of keys.

"Three night!" she screeched, holding up her thumb and first two fingers. "Bed!" She opened a door and gestured toward the room with the same acerbic tone and furrowed brow. "Bath!" she pointed toward another door at the end of the hall. With that, she pounded back down the stairs and was gone.

"I'm too tired to even be scared of that right now," I told Pema.

We collapsed onto the mattresses, desperate to be horizontal. We didn't care that they were on the floor or notice that the water taps were broken. Except for the fifteen-foot-high ceilings with flaking decorative trim, the room was unimpressive. Plaster patches marred the walls, and a bent wire hanger hung from a nail in the middle of the far wall, as though it were a piece of art. A dead plant sat on a small table draped in a sticky flowered plastic tablecloth. Dust coated a bare bulb, which hung from the ceiling by a single electrical wire that stretched high around the room.

The sound of scooters woke me late in the afternoon. I opened the wooden shutters and hung out the window, wearing only my tie-dye T-shirt. Tile-roofed buildings stretched across the town toward hazy mountains and bell towers in the distance. For the first time in weeks, it felt like it had been worth the effort to get here. I had a good feeling about it. Pema snapped a picture of my bare ass.

We headed down the street ready to gorge ourselves on the first thing we found. Colossal prawns, olives, feta, beer!

"Do you want to keep that room?" Pema broached the subject after we were seated.

"Yes, it's just a place to crash, after all. Not like we're going to spend any time there. I'd rather save my money for some decent meals for once," I said, licking my fingers and draining the beer.

"Hmm. I don't know if I'm willing to stay. I think it's beyond disgusting and not even a good price," Pema said.

"Let's see if we can find something else first before we give it up."

"Deal," Pema agreed.

We found the King Otheon Hotel around the corner listed in the visitor's guide. It had a charming room available for only 3,400 drachmas more (about $20, so only $10 each) and a bougainvillea-filled courtyard where we could take our breakfasts.

"Who's going to tell the old crone we're leaving early?" I asked. "She scares me. Did you hear her yelling last night? She must've been drunk. Slamming and banging around."

"Seriously? No, I must've slept through it," Pema said.

I rolled my eyes and bit my tongue. All the girl ever did was sleep, for Christ's sake.

"What?" Pema asked.

My irritation wasn't lost on her.

"Nothing. It was just really creepy."

"I'll tell her," Pema offered. "Tomorrow."

"And get our passports back too," I reminded her.

...

We met Chuck and his friend Giorgos, a local, at an outdoor cafe. It was a welcome relief to distract ourselves with some company other than our own. The two men caught up after not having seen each other in ages. Giorgo had pursed lips and an affected British accent that came and went over the course of the evening. He sprinkled deprecating comments about women into the conversation while he petted my bare shoulder and thigh. I hated his little round glasses and giant thick eyebrows. His hair was perfectly shaped, and he wore a preppy Izod shirt. In spite of his Greek hairiness and dense build, there was something feminine about him, school-boyish and wide-hipped.

Pema and I read each other's minds and kicked each other under the table, stifling our laughter.

"*Stronzo!*" I mouthed to her. *Turd*. We burst out laughing, unable to contain ourselves.

"Fishing accident," Chuck said, raising his three-fingered hand, oblivious to our laughter, when he saw the sideways glances we snuck at it. Our eyes widened, imagining a gruesome accident. Chuck guffawed loudly, took his hat off and whipped the table with it, his body bouncing up and down on his chair from his laughter. "*No, I'm not drunk!*" he shouted with an exaggerated hillbilly accent as he continued laughing. He knew exactly what we were thinking—that he was crazy drunk. But in fact there was a soda sitting in front of him.

"Oh, it gets them every time," Chuck said and finally put his cap back on, tucking the wild strays up into it.

After dinner, Chuck wandered off in a daze, apparently his MO, according to Giorgos, who told us Chuck lived in a world of his own, and we followed Giorgos to Koraki, a favorite bar with the locals. A blue neon sign hung above the single door, casting a dreamlike haze on the entrance. Dark, crowded, and cavelike, techno disco music slammed out of the speakers, and cigarette smoke spilled out the door following a small crowd of drinkers into the alley. The bartender was tall with a shaved head and a body like Adonis. I was drawn to him the minute I walked in the door, as though my energy was sucked through a vortex directly to him. We all wedged into a small space at the bar.

"Thof, meet my friends Niki and Pema," Giorgos yelled over the commotion to the bartender, showing us off like two fillies, his hands on our shoulders.

"I know you from somewhere." The bartender's eyes bored into mine.

"You've got to be kidding me."

"No, I'm serious," he said. "We know each other. Maybe it was another lifetime, but we do know each other. Are you a writer?"

Pema and I look at each other, eyes wide. "She is!" Pema answered for me.

"I am not!" I blurted.

"She's writing a book, but she doesn't admit it to anyone," Pema continued. "All she does is write. Never takes her head out of her journals."

And all you do is sleep and eat chocolate, I thought.

Pema had bought boxes of chocolate in Austria weeks earlier, intending to ship them home to her family as presents, but the weight of them in her backpack had become too much and they were melting fast. She systematically began to eat them, bringing a box along on the day trips we took. One day on the way to Epidaurus she dozed off with the box melting on her lap. Her stomach jiggled, and her shirt grew rings of sweat, attracting the leers of fellow bus passengers. I glared back at them, trying to protect her dignity, wanting to wake her, but too embarrassed for her. It was easier for both of us to let her sleep through it.

"Well, if he claims to know me, then be my guest! Ooh la la," I whisper-yelled over the music into Pema's ear.

"Come to the boat tonight. I'm having a few people over for drinks when I get off," Thof shouted.

"You girls go—I have to be at work in the morning. I've seen how these things end and it's usually not pretty," Giorgos said with a chuckle and a wink to Thof.

Pema and I looked at each other in silent agreement. "Sure! Where's your boat?"

"You know where the south harbor is? It's the third slip, on the second ramp. Her name's *Ponirose*. Giorgos can point you in the right direction."

"Pony Rose? What kind of name is that for a boat?" I asked him sarcastically.

"*Poh*-nee-ros. It means foxy," Thof explained.

"Whew. Okay, then; we'll come." Pema and I nodded in unison. "And by the way, what kind of name is Thof?" I asked.

"Theodore Oswald Fiomako. I'm quite the mutt. My mother's a Brit, my father a Greek. They didn't last long and neither did the name," he shouted.

"What do they do?"

"Ugo, my father, is in the ouzo business. His family has been making it for three generations. Two years ago he opened a new shop right in the middle of town. Mom was a schoolteacher. She died eight years ago," he told me.

"Oh, I'm so sorry," I said, feeling more uncomfortable with all he was telling me than actually feeling empathetic.

"Thanks. She didn't want to be here. She had psychotic episodes. They became more and more frequent, and she wouldn't stay on her meds. There was nothing we could do," he told me as he carried a pile of plates to the sink.

"Gawd. Did she…?" Why was he telling me this? I wondered. It's as though he really did know me from some past life.

"Yeah. She ODed on psychotropics she'd been hoarding. God knows where she got them. There were a few dark, painful years leading up to it. It makes you grateful for the present moment. On a brighter note… Dad also started producing wines again and they're getting some attention now.

"Costa!" he yelled to the other bartender, ending the conversation as abruptly as he started it, "Can you close tonight, buddy? I wanna check out early."

"Nothing ever changes." Costa, so dark and pretty, rolled his eyes and winked at us. "Sure, buddy. Anything for you."

"Costa here's my right-hand man," Thof told me, introducing us. "I don't know what I'd do without him, do I, Costa?" Thof winked at Costa and punched him on the arm.

After a few drinks, Giorgos walked with us to an outdoor cafe where we killed time waiting for Thof. It was midnight and the square was full of people, mostly tourists and families with children racing around as though they'd just been let loose from being tied up all day. The breeze came in off the water. It was glorious after the blazing heat and humidity of the day. We ordered iced coffees with a little sugar—*metrios*—and sat watching the people until Giorgos finally begged off.

"It was sweet of him to hook us up, but my gawd, what a dolt." Pema commented on Giorgos.

"I get first dibs on the bartender," I joked.

"He's all yours."

"There's something about him…" I trailed off, knowing it was risky territory saying that to Pema. She wouldn't approve. "His mother died, committed suicide," I added. "Does it seem odd that he told me that?"

"Maybe that's his schtick." Pema seemed bored and tired. She had a way of suddenly changing her moods—from pensive and dark to cheerful and talkative. Like when she struck up a conversation with Chuck on the bus ride to Nafplio. I never knew when her mood would turn on a dime.

I sensed she didn't like my interest in Thof or what it might lead to. She knew firsthand what I'd given up being married to Jin for the last five years. She was the only person I told everything to. But since Pema lost the baby she and Bing had shortly after they'd gotten married, our relationship was never quite the same. I was always looking for a way to get it back. I hoped asking her to come on the trip would mend some of that. She still held a grudge against me for refusing to take care of Jin's mother while she was grieving. It was true—I hadn't helped—and I still felt bad about it. I had no idea what Pema was going through at the time but was determined not to take that kind of order from Jin and refused to wait hand and foot on his mother.

No one knew at the time of our wedding that Jin's mother had bought a one-way ticket, all the way from Malaysia, where Jin and younger Bing grew up. "What a waste it would be to fly all this way only to turn around and go back," she announced. She had a habit of dropping bombs with no concern about how it affected anyone else. So Jin found her an apartment a half mile down the road, where she had nothing to do and nowhere to go. He instructed me to look after her while he was at work. I may have been naïve, but I also had a mind of my own and would never agree to that. It earned me the first of many black marks. So it fell to Bing. Bing, who had anger management problems, immediately pawned his mother off onto pregnant Pema. Since she was the first daughter-in-law, the burden of caretaking would remain forever on her shoulders, even after she and Bing divorced.

If anything were to happen between Thof and me, Bing would find out fast, and he would tell Jin. I changed the subject to plans for our next and last stop, Santorini. Pema was excited to show me around the blue-domed buildings and steep winding streets.

As we approached Thof's boat, laughter rose from the docks. "You sure you wanna do this?" Pema asked.

"Oh, why not? It seems safe enough. He's Giorgos' friend." I was surprised at myself.

Maybe it was the drinks at the bar or the cooling air. I didn't usually go for group things, always feeling somehow an outsider. I was an observer.

"And we've known Giorgos for all of eight hours…" Pema hesitated again.

"Knock, knock." I said rapping on the side of the boat.

"Hey! I'm so glad you came. Let me help you in." Thof jumped up and took our hands as we climbed over the edge into the rocking boat.

"Everyone, this is Niki and Pema. They're Giorgos' friends. Metaxa? Margarita? Beer?" Thof offered.

"Ooh, Metaxa, *parakalo*," I said, still a little high from the drinks we had at the bar. The coffee had barely taken the edge off.

"Margarita for me, *efaristo*," Pema said.

Thof's friends switched their conversations to mostly English, but we still only understood half of it. The drunken, exaggerated storytelling was funny enough without having to understand it all.

"How was your travel here?" one of them asked us in broken English. Pema and I looked at each other and burst out laughing.

"*Cosi brutto!*" I said. *So ugly.* "Pema, tell them about the wonderful night on the ferry."

"You wouldn't believe the group of drunk Italians," she started. "They harassed anyone within sight, screaming, yelling, and clapping. It was a sleepless night."

"I was so mad I yelled at them *Vaffanculo, teste di cazzo!—Fuck off, dick heads*—then hid my head under my coat."

The Italian street slang book I'd bought as a joke turned out to be one of the best things I'd brought with me. Pema and I would practice the most inane sayings and crack up laughing when one of us blurted out a phrase in the middle of dinner or on the train. It helped ease the growing tension between us.

> *Soo sbronzo. I'm totally wasted.*
>
> *Il mio vicino e flippato e dovrebbe andare*
>
> *da uno strizzacervelli! My neighbor's nuts and*
>
> *should go see a shrink!*
>
> *Lo facciamo alla pecorina? Wanna do it*
>
> *doggy-style?*
>
> *Hai cambiato le tue biancheria intima*
>
> *oggi? Did you change your underwear today?*

I felt a tingling in my stomach like an electrical current when my eyes met Thof's from across the boat. He smiled and raised his eyebrows mischievously as if he knew what I had felt. He nodded and the biggest grin I'd ever seen spread across his face.

"What's going on?" Pema asked me.

"I don't know, but I feel kind of breathless."

"I think Thof wants you." Pema elbowed me. "*Colpo di fulmine!*" *A thunderbolt of love!*

"Mamma mia!" I snorted back, cracking up. Gawd, it was good to laugh. Maybe this last leg of our trip could be resurrected. I had a good feeling.

Thof's friends continued into the night with their boisterous stories. Laughter could be heard all around the harbor from other boats, all lit up with string lights. We cracked crabs, pulling the meat out of their claws until we were satiated, and screamed when someone pointed to a shooting star.

The gentle swaying of the boat was turning my stomach upside down, though. I could get motion sickness at the mere mention of it. The fishy smell of the harbor and the crab juice running down my arms suddenly took a turn for the worse and I had the sudden urge to heave.

"I'm going to be sick!" I blurted.

"Whoa! Everybody out!" Thof laughed. They must have done this drill before. Everyone kept their seats and cheered me out of the boat, raising their glasses to me.

I stumbled over to the edge, banging my shin on the step as I leaped out and hung my head over the other side of the dock. Luckily, I managed to swallow back the bile and not completely embarrass myself.

"Let me walk you two back to your hotel," Thof offered, waving his friends goodnight.

"Good idea. Whooo! That was too close for comfort," I said. Thank gawd I didn't make a total fool of myself. "A walk will do me good."

"Where's your hotel?"

"It's no hotel; just a room," I said.

"That's an understatement!" Pema added.

"What's it called?" Thof asked.

"There's no name. Just some old woman's room above her shop. We're moving to King Otheon tomorrow."

The three of us walked arm in arm through the winding

alleys. My arm was hot and tingling where Thof's arm hooked around mine. My entire body buzzed and hummed. He smiled and nodded knowingly.

"Oh, crap. This place?" Thof said as we approached the old woman's shop. "It's good you found another place."

"You know it?" Pema asked.

"Everyone knows everyone here, believe me. This woman is nuts," Thof told us, and he jokingly howled at the moon.

"I want to show you something," Thof whispered in my ear.

"What?" I asked.

"You'll know it when you see. You've seen it before."

"Right, uh-huh—just like 'we've met before.'"

I didn't want the evening to end. I turned to Pema who was heading up the stairs.

"Pema, do you mind if Thof and I keep walking? I need more air to get rid of the swaying. I'll catch up with you soon."

I saw the disappointment on her face and knew I'd have to make up for it later, but now the universe was taking over. It felt the most natural thing in the world to go with Thof, a virtual stranger, as though the script was already written. Pema sulked up the stairs to our room.

We left the lights of the street and took the winding cobblestone alley up the hill, into the darkness. Beach scrub pines clung to the hillside, gradually overtaking the ancient-looking stone houses. I'd never heard crickets so loud. It was as though an orchestra was serenading us.

"It's because of the full moon," Thof said.

"What is?"

"Why the crickets are so loud."

I stopped abruptly, facing him. There was that current again. He kissed me gently, but it felt like a tiny bee sting.

"I can't believe this," I said.

"I can."

The Aegean Sea lapped calmly at the beach below. Above, 999 steps led to Palamidi, a seventeenth-century fortress on the cliff. The full moon was so bright I could see the blueness of the water and the spiny urchins clinging to rocks in the shallow pools far below.

We tripped and stumbled down the rocky path talking and laughing all the way—amazing talk that only ever seems to happen when you first meet someone. I told him all about Jin and how I couldn't believe I would soon be going home. What had I learned? What decisions had I made? I was empty and alone. I'd been alone for years, begging to be heard. Am I so broken that I don't deserve it?

As though it was the most natural thing in the world, we slipped our clothes off and dipped into the water, carefully avoiding the spiny urchins. My head was spinning with conflicting thoughts. Could I cheat on Jin? I deserved to be fulfilled now, to be touched by a lover. This man was a stranger, but it really did feel like I'd known him in another lifetime. What would Pema think? Why was I more concerned with Pema than my own husband? Maybe because I'd have to face her in the morning—her silence, her depression. Jin, I could put out of my mind for the time being.

We spent the rest of the night making love on the rooftop of Thof's apartment. At first, I felt paralyzed, but he was gentle and patient, and my natural instincts took over as a tingling current moved through my body. I'd never felt anything like it before. Raw energy.

For the next four days, Pema and I tiptoed around the elephant in the room. We read our books, shopped, hung out at Koraki until late every night, then I disappeared until the morning. It was never mentioned between us.

Thof and I made love in six-hour stretches, every inch of our bodies repelling and attracting like magnets, holding back or exploding our orgasms. We kept going from when he got off work until sunrise. My muscles spasmed from exhaustion and dehydration, and I was nearly hallucinating. In between stints we talked more—about relationships, Nietzsche, quantum mechanics, the meaning of life. Had Jin and I ever talked about that? About anything meaningful?

And day after day, Thof coached me on channeling my energy, as he said he'd done the first moment he saw me, at the bar.

"That's what you felt," he said.

I wanted to be skeptical, but I knew what he said was true.

One day, sitting beside each other in what had quickly become our favorite lunch spot, a Japanese ramen shop, of all things, I "pushed" a current of energy through him, making him jump.

"Fucking hell! You felt that, didn't you?" I asked excitedly.

"Do it again," he challenged me. And I did.

"You have so much power you have no clue," he told me. "You're going to be famous someday, you know, writing your books."

"What else do you know about me that I don't?"

"I can't tell you anything else, my little cubby; it's too soon."

"Oh puh-leeze, you're being so woo-woo. Knock it off and tell me." But he wouldn't and left me wondering.

We ordered our usual, the shoyu ramen with raw quail egg and wakame, and proceeded to make a spectacle of ourselves in spite of sitting in the dark corner booth in the very back of the restaurant.

"Pass the egg, please," I said.

Other patrons tried not to look as we passed the raw yolk back and forth directly between our mouths. He pressed his mouth firmly against mine so the yolk didn't break until we were ready. Bursting it between our tongues, it oozed into both of our mouths. He pulled away and I licked the sweet, sticky yellow off his lips, dripping warm.

3

Pema and I had repacked our backpacks and moved to the Hotel King Otheon before even telling the old woman. We knew she spent her days in the shop below our room. When we arrived, we heard chatter toward the back. The shop looked like a secondhand junk store and had the prices of a high-end boutique. Dust coated all the dishes and platters; some were even chipped. There were hand-painted dish towels and giant wooden spoons with gaudy scenes of famous Greek landmarks and replicas of statuaries. We made our way to the back, Pema leading the way. I carried the backpacks—I wore mine on my back and I bear-hugged Pema's as though it was a shield.

Three figures in faded black smocks, black scarves, black shoes and hose sat at a small table in theback where the darkened shop opened up to a private courtyard, perfectly framed by an archway with a backdrop of bright red bougainvillea and white stone. They turned in unison when they heard our footsteps. Pema stopped short and I bumped into her back. Staring back at us were three mustachioed old women. They looked like Giorgos!

Thank gawd Pema had agreed to be the front man.

"*Chairete.*" *Hello*. Pema said this so softly that even I, right on her back, hardly heard. The three old man-ladies nodded in unison.

"We need to leave early; we've decided to stay at a friend's place," Pema told the old woman. "So, uh, we'll need our passports back."

"You stay three nights," the woman barked.

"We're really sorry, but we've been invited to a friend's house," Pema said. I was surprised to hear her lie. We hadn't discussed what she'd say.

The old lady translated what Pema said to the other women around the table. "Thof, the bar owner, has invited us to stay with him." Pema added another lie.

Thof was the only word I understood the old lady say as she told her friends what Pema said, and much more. Gasps erupted around the table.

"Thof. *Alepou!*" the old woman shouted at Pema and the three of them crossed themselves in unison. We took half a step back.

The old woman stood up abruptly without consulting her friends and shoved passed us, moving faster than it looked like she could possibly move. She pressed a key on the old-fashioned cash register, and the drawer popped open with a *ching*. She fished the passports out from the back of the drawer, slammed it shut with more clatter, and slapped the passports down on the counter.

"Go! Get away! *Keres!*" she hollered, pointing toward the door. She returned to her friends, who made clucking sounds and shook their heads.

We practically ran out of the shop, barely avoiding crashing into the pottery and knickknacks with our unwieldy backpacks.

"I told you she was crazy! What the hell did she say?" I asked Pema.

"Shit! They're like a coven!" Pema said.

"What did they call Thof? *Al-a-poo?*"

"Hell if I know. And what's a *Keres?*" Pema asked.

"Let's get a drink," I said.

"Well, hello! Ho ho ho, girls!" came a greeting from the bar. "And so we meet again!"

The place was fuller than we expected, since it was only early afternoon. A new load of tourists must have arrived from a cruise ship.

Thof began the introductions. "Meet Niki and Pema, my new friends. Chuck, behave yourself." Thof winked at me.

"Oh yes, we go way back," I said, Pema and I rolling our eyes at each other.

"Sorry there aren't two seats together, ladies. Looks like you'll have to sit one on either side of me. Booyah!" Chuck was clearly entertained with himself.

"*Ti amo ancora di più oggi.*" *I love you even more today.* I whispered this sexily to Pema and shot a glance at Chuck. *Not!* we mouthed simultaneously behind his back.

"My sailboat's in the yard," he told us, bringing up his boat again. "You two should come take a look. I'm there working on it all the time. Gonna be leaving soon, though. Yup! Should only be a week or two now. Gonna take her round to Corsica. You girls could come along if you like! We'll have a party! All that and a bag of chips!" His laughter started all over again with the same self-amusement.

"Alrighty then," Pema said, and we exchanged looks again.

"Thof, we had a little run-in with your friend the old witch with the pottery shop." I winked at Pema.

"Oh yeah, Thof. She's a good friend of yours, huh?" Pema asked as he walked away to wipe down the other end of the bar.

"That old crone," Chuck horned in. "She and her coven—those old prunes can suck my dick. Bunch of crazy bitches. Ha!" he said, taking his cap off to lash the bar with it, and giving his soda a loud slurp.

"Ew." I imagined the three old mustachioed women kneeling in front of him. Thof busied himself with other customers across the room, ignoring us.

"The first time they saw me they about fainted." Chuck ping-ponged his head back and forth from Pema to me. "They huddled together like a bunch of nervous geese and waddled away as fast as their hairy legs could carry them. They still give me the stink eye every time they see me." Chuck scratched his head.

"Well, they sure chased us out of there today when we told them we were leaving early. At the mention of Thof's name you'd think it was the devil we were talking about." Thof turned toward us frowning while he took a customer's order.

"Do you know what *Keres* means?" Pema asked Chuck. "Or *al-a-poo*?"

"Ooh, you really did scare them. Woohoo! You she-devils! Better than blazed!" Chuck closed his eyes and rolled his head around.

"Stevie Wonder?" I asked Chuck.

"Linda Blair!" Chuck snorted. "C'mon girls!"

"Does anyone understand anything you say?" Pema asked him.

"Thof!" Chuck yelled across the room. "Come over here and take our picture. I want to remember this day."

"Sure, Chuck," Thof said, balancing a pile of dirty plates on his arm and wiping down a table with the other hand while taking an order from yet another table. "Just as soon as I'm done with my cigarette break here I'll run right over. Customers." He rolled his eyes and pretended to laugh.

"I think he's busy, Chuck," I said.

"Nah, he ain't." Chuck rolled his eyes back at Thof. "So, *Keres*… you asked… female spirits of cruel death, like from war, murder, or ravaging disease. I guess that's what you become if you hang out with our Thof, that fox. *Alepou* means fox."

"Charming," Pema said. "How do you know that?"

"I sold encyclopedias door to door to put myself through college. It wasn't a total waste of time," Chuck explained. "There are some old rumors about our Thof here. I'll leave it up to you two to ask him. Fanged, taloned women, dressed in bloody garments. Yup, that's you two. Thof! Picture!" Chuck yelled again.

"Damn it, Chuck," Thof said under his breath, dumping the dirty dishes in the sink.

"Thof, why did she call us *Keres* and you a fox after we mentioned your name?" I asked.

"They even crossed themselves, for Christ's sake!" Pema said.

"Why did you mention my name?" Thof scowled.

"Oh, now you're opening up Pandora's box, girls," Chuck said. "Look that one up. Ha!"

"Just ignore the old lady. Ignore Chuck!" Thof said irritably. "They're a bunch of harmless old superstitious women with too much time on their hands."

"They were pretty serious," Pema said. "Like something had happened."

"Listen, sorry, but I have to keep up with the customers; they're starting to get impatient." Thof turned abruptly and left us alone again with Chuck.

"What's wrong with him all of the sudden?" Chuck asked.

Somehow Chuck and Giorgos stuck to us like dog hair on a sweater, and the five of us spent our days playing in the ocean. Thof and I napped on the rocky beach to catch up on lost sleep from our nightly expeditions into transcendent sex. The water was so salty, it was buoyant. I felt like an egg, cracked open and dropped into the water. My fingers and toes, like the whites of the egg, drifted away from the yolk of my body. Floating there, I had a vision. Hundreds of years in the past, I'd been here, at this beach, looking up at the top of the empty cliff where there was no fortress yet. I was a messenger, clothed in sheepskins, hiking the mountains, delivering information from village to village. Except for a skulk of fox who protected and guided me, I traveled alone and was regarded throughout the land as an all-knowing soul. The vision flashed in my mind in an instant and was gone just as fast, yet held an entire lifetime.

Now I'd finally returned to this forgotten place and to this heavenly creature who knew my past and future. But there was a darkness, too, right under the surface, shallow like the roots of the scrub pines barely holding on to the rocky cliff. I wondered what the old woman in the shop knew about Thof.

Meanwhile, Pema was fit to be tied. Sulking, eating, napping, sweating. I tried to include her, but she was in a world of her own—as was I, if truth be told. Thof invited a friend along to the beach one day to "play" with Pema. That was a strange word choice, I thought, but chalked it up to his rough English and hoped for the best. Pema was offended at the man's fatness—a perfect reflection of her own—as he pawed at her while trying to navigate his sputtering little boat around the lagoon. He was clueless. Pema sat at the stern frowning. She couldn't understand a word he said.

By midafternoon it was too hot to be on the beach. Thof would leave for work at Koraki and finally Pema had me to herself for day excursions to the ruins of Mycenae, an ancient stone theater in the middle of nowhere, or to the ancient town of Delphi. The heat was oppressive and the tours boring.

We'd been in Nafplio an entire week. By far the longest we'd stayed in one place, and our last night approached. I was panicked at the thought of leaving Thof, and full of dread over heading back to Jin. After Santorini, we'd be flying to Rome to catch our plane home.

"Marry me," Thof said over coffee. We'd become regulars at Sokaki Cafe. It was rustic with dark corners to hide in.

"I'm already married!" I laughed. "That's pretty funny."

"I'll wait."

He wasn't kidding.

I didn't want to go home to Jin, and I also didn't want to get married again—maybe ever.

...

My wedding to Jin had been a small affair in the chapel of the Lutheran church on the campus of the state university where we were attending college. My parents and brother and sister flew in from the East Coast, Jin's family from the Far East.

His mother was a manic-depressive, recently recovered from electroshock treatments, which her ex-husband, Jin's father, who was a doctor, had prescribed. The treatments left her catatonic and whimpering.

My mother, an acerbic, pragmatic woman, was put out at having to fly across the country to witness my wedding to an "Oriental" man. "You better not let him tell you what to do," her wedding advice to me was. "Because you know that's what *those* people do." My father, who had no agenda and simply wanted everyone to be happy, was charming and teary-eyed.

Jin's father arrived at the wedding mistress-less for the first time I'd ever seen. On trips we'd taken back to Jin's home, his father always had a long-haired beauty on his arm. He seemed more interested in taunting Jin's mother with the women than actually relating to whomever he was with. The women and Jin's mother would get into cat fights in the middle of a restaurant. Jin and his brother pretended nothing was happening as conversations around us stopped and people stared. I was alone in my shock and embarrassment. Apparently, if no one acknowledged it, then it never happened.

Bing, with his permanent expression of irritation, and Pema, his pregnant wife at the time, were also in attendance at our wedding. They had recently gotten married purely for the baby's sake, with no intention of it lasting. It didn't and tragically, neither did the baby.

The only nonfamilial guest at our wedding was Holly, Jin's good friend, who I suspected had slept with him not so long before, and who had not been invited. Yet there she stood, in line with the families. She wore a white puffy dress, which made her look like a midget virgin. Over top of the dress she wore Jin's denim jacket—my favorite. I never did get that jacket back. The bitch. I glared at her.

If I'd had it my way, we would've had the ceremony in some field, but since my parents were paying, they insisted on a church wedding. We got away with having it in the chapel, at least, instead of the nave, and it would be on a Tuesday, the only day the church would fit us in since we weren't members—God's lower class.

I'd bought my dress—a white, strapless cocktail-looking getup—at a trendy clothing store downtown. Jin wore a suit with a bow tie. Dashing as ever. Moments before I walked down the aisle (a hallway), Jin's mother presented me with the thick, gaudy gold necklace and insisted I replace my pearls (fake) with it. I didn't care how expensive the chain surely was, I hated it, but I kowtowed anyway. It hung around my neck like a heavy snake, serpentine and glinting, and became the focal point in every single picture.

It was a short and sweet ceremony. I wasn't interested in the least with God's opinion about it. Cutting the cake, the sun shone down on Jin and me—a stunning picture of innocence, our bright futures ahead of us. And that was that. My family flew home. Bing, Pema, and I went to classes the next day, and Jin went back to work. It was as though nothing had happened.

...

I thought about calling Jin now and telling him I was staying in Nafplio, but my gawd, how could I do that to him? You don't just run away and not come back, I told myself. This wasn't a Hollywood movie. I needed to do the responsible thing. Go home and settle it between Jin and me, face to face. My thoughts flip-flopped between the fantasy and the consequences of staying in Nafplio. My own family would shame me over a divorce (except my sister, who would secretly be jealous), and I would certainly be on Jin's family's blacklist. It's not like I could tell them about his perversion. Pema was the only one who knew. I could feel myself starting to tear up.

"Don't worry; you'll be back. It won't be long," Thof said, wrapping me in his arms.

"How do you know? How can I leave you? I feel reborn since we met—sexually, intellectually, spiritually. Like the possibilities are endless. Isn't that the meaning of life? I had been sleepwalking with Jin. He was a fantasy of my own making that never materialized.

"You've awakened me; we're fire together. It's animal," I told Thof.

"Trust me, you'll be back. And while we're apart we'll feel each other's energy, just like I taught you."

"But that's not enough. I can't believe it's come to this."

"Give me that coin off your bracelet," he told me.

I'd been collecting charms since the beginning of our trip. "The Greek one?" I asked him.

"Yes," he said and unhooked it from the links. "I'm going to keep this and by the time we see each other again, it will be smooth because every time I think of you, I'll rub it and send you my energy. You'll see."

Pema joined us in the coffee shop for breakfast. "What's wrong, Niki? You need to get your stuff packed."

I forced a smile. Grow up, Niki, I told myself. You're not sixteen. You got yourself into this; life goes on.

"Right. I know," I pouted, alone in my thoughts. I knew Pema could see right through it, but neither one of us mentioned it.

4

The train station was empty of travelers but full of flies. On the platform, elderly village men with potbellies and bushy ear hair sat chatting in rickety chairs in the sun, passing time in the oppressive heat. They smiled, eyeing us as we lugged our backpacks down the antiquated platform one last time. On the train, wrinkled, sun-darkened men with white toothy smiles walked up and down the aisle, car to car, hawking trays of souvlaki carried high above their heads, shouting in competition with one another. It smelled wonderful. We ordered four from a little man, which seemed to make him very happy.

Following the Isthmus of Corinth, the train slogged its way to Athens, tooting its horn at every crossroad. At one, a father and his son sat together on an old bicycle, waving and watching as though the passing train was a rare treat. Goats were tied in people's backyards. A lone donkey stood under an olive tree. Lemon trees, short and round, dangled bright yellow fruit. The train stopped in a small village for no known reason. A conductor wearing white socks in sandals walked up and down the platform holding a stick with a green circle on it, perhaps a signal to the conductor. A priest dressed in a black cassock talked to a woman as a rooster raced past them across the platform. I wrote it all down in my journal.

...

It was open seating on the plane from Athens to Santorini, and people pushed, shoved, and elbowed their way to find a seat. There were only twelve. It wasn't like one seat was safer or closer to the exit than another. The entire plane was so small it made no difference. Front. Back. Middle. It was all within an arm's reach. Headrests were wrapped with electrical tape to keep the stuffing in. I wondered what other parts of the plane were held together with it.

The miracle of takeoff happened as the rattling and moaning vibration of the plane sent my seat into spasms. No one else seemed to mind the roller-coaster ride we had embarked on. They all shouted over the sound of the engine. Pema managed to fall asleep while I tried to distract myself with a magazine and told myself, mantra-like, that I hadn't met Thof, my omniscient soulmate, only to go down in flames over the Mediterranean.

Santorini was picture-perfect, exactly like the brochures promised, which helped keep my mind off Thof for about a second. I tried to be present with Pema, but my mind was on him, and I could hardly keep from crying.

"Are you going to go on like this, Niki? You're acting like a brokenhearted teenager. Can't you enjoy what's right in front of you? It makes me feel like chopped liver. I've been playing third wheel for the entire last week."

I responded in silence. If I talked, I would cry.

A skinny stick of a little girl stepped off the street and onto our small slate patio. She had stringy hair and bony knees and was wearing a dirty shirt. She held a watermelon in front of her in her interlaced fingers and chattered away in a language indecipherable to us, swaying the watermelon back and forth like a dance partner.

"Money?" was the only word we understood as she held the melon out to us. Her smile was mesmerizing. She chattered on and on, completely oblivious to the fact that we didn't understand a word she said.

Pema and I traded looks between ourselves and this elfish creature.

"*Maria!*" a woman's voice called out from somewhere down the street. The girl turned serious. She handed the melon to me and reached out a hand, palm up.

"Got any coins?" I asked Pema. We both dug around in our pockets and handed a few to the girl, which sent her jumping and skipping down the street.

It had been enough distraction to change the mood and avoid the subject.

That night we found Tony's, an outdoor bar, overlooking the Sea of Crete. We drank Metaxa under the stars while the Gipsy Kings played over the speakers. It was a glorious night.

"I'm tired of being nauseated from all the cigarette smoke. You can never get away from it—trains, restaurants, sidewalks," I complained woozily as clouds of smoke wafted past.

"If you can't beat 'em, join 'em," Pema said.

"No way."

"Way! Do it. It's the only way to get over it and stop being so mad about it." She handed me her pack of cigarettes and lighter. She carried a pack in her back pocket when we went out at night as an icebreaker to meeting people, always able to offer them a light if asked. She had only smoked a few times on the entire trip. "I dare you," she said.

"I'm drunk enough to take you up on that. But you light it for me." I was swooning at the absurdity of actually smoking a cigarette. Both my parents had been chain-smokers until they finally quit when I was a teenager and took up bike riding, vegetarianism, and recycling, all before they were "things." If they knew what I was about to do they'd have a fit. Since I was old enough to understand, I'd bitched and complained about their cigarette smoke—how disgusting it was and how nauseated it made me. Now I was about to eat my words.

Pema lit one up for herself, then took another out of the pack, lit it from hers, and handed it to me. By the end of the evening she'd taken a picture of me with two lit cigarettes hanging from my lips trying my best not to laugh.

"Oh my gawd! Jin would not approve!" I blurted out.

"I'm sure that's the least of your worries," Pema said.

"Ouch! Thanks for that," I said. Why did she have to ruin the vibe? "They're closing, I'm going back to the room." I left her sitting there by herself.

Jin hadn't approved of so many things about me—the belly dancing troupe I'd joined in a desperate attempt to find a tribe of my own after we got married and moved to the city, and much less the navel piercing I got as a result. It didn't help matters when at my birthday party, friends surprised me with a cake decorated with a silver ring dripping with fake blood. Jin had no idea what it meant until I revealed my piercing.

The next morning Pema and I slept late and in silence, nursed our hangovers with strong, sweet coffee and a greasy breakfast. Still not speaking to each other, we headed out to the beach. When we couldn't stand the heat anymore, we got a bus back to town, bought more salami and bread, cut into the watermelon, had a siesta, and started all over again at Tony's, barely speaking to each other.

It was early in the evening Greek time, only 11:30. "*Buona sera i miei amori!*" Tony, the owner, greeted us.

Only a few people were inside, some friends of Tony's, who were part of the smoke-blowing crowd the night before. We hesitated, trying to decide where to sit.

"A bar too empty is as difficult as a bar too full," Tony laughed. We sat at the bar.

"It's Roman's birthday today," Tony announced, pointing his chin at one of his friends and presenting the four of us each with red, cough-syrup-looking liquid in a thimble.

"Can you make a screaming orgasm?" Pema asked out

of character, after we all gagged down the red syrup. This became the topic of conversation for the rest of the evening. The place filled up, and the air became even thicker with cigarette smoke. The night dragged on with champagne and flirting. Pema made a chair for Roman out of the champagne wire and presented it to him on her outstretched palm as though it was a gold ring. "I accept this with honor," Roman winked at Pema.

The moon was about to burst in its fullness. Dogs barked in the distance as though they were laughing. I couldn't get Thof out of my head.

The next morning we were both greeted with yet another hangover and headed out in search of coffee again.

"What's wrong? You seem more than hungover. Is it the ashtray mouth or are you jealous that I was the one having a good time last night?" Pema asked me in a rare moment of honesty.

"I want to leave early and go back to Nafplio," I said.

"Great, Niki. Another wrestling match to get our passports back early again? And we don't have the money to fly back, so another twelve hours on stinking boats and buses all for the sake of Thof? Shit."

She lit a cigarette and slammed the lighter onto the table, rattling our coffee cups.

"I'm really sorry. I understand if you want to stay. Catch up with me in Nafplio so we can go to the airport together for the flight home."

"It's not that I want to stay here; it's that I'd rather be alone than with you guys. You two suck the air out the room."

"I get it. I'm sorry. It's just that… well, it sounds so ridiculous, but I can't even begin to tell you how it feels."

"Yeah, yeah, yeah. Whatever," Pema said. "You go. I may even try to get out of here early and fly home."

"There's Roman and his friends; they're fun. You could hang out with them. Roman sure likes you." I tried to keep it upbeat.

"Right." Pema gave me a sarcastic smile. "I'll be fine,

Niki. Don't worry about me. Who knows? Maybe you'll decide not to come home."

"Believe me, I've already thought about that. I made a list of pros and cons."

Pema rolled her eyes. "You do what you want. You always do."

"Promise you'll call me and let me know what your plans are, okay? I'll worry about you if I don't hear from you," I said.

"Sure thing." Pema stubbed out her cigarette and went back to the room.

5

For the second time I was elbow to elbow on a ferry with a crowd of hot, dirty, loud-mouthed travelers, but this time I was alone. If one more person blew smoke in my face or dumped their ashes on me, I'd scream *Stronzo!*—*assholes*—I thought, and started to cry. If Pema had been there, we would have found a way to laugh. Would she ever speak to me again? Would I ever see her again?

After eight hours, the ferry only got me as far as Piraeus. From there I'd have to get on a different ferry to Poros, then a bus to cross the peninsula to Argos, then a short walk to Nafplio. This kind of travel had become unbearable. If it wasn't gagging on cigarette smoke, it was choking on carbon monoxide spewing from buses. If it wasn't the smell of toilets, it was the smell of garbage. If it wasn't garbage, it was dog shit. If not dog shit, more cigarette smoke. If it wasn't cigarette smoke, it was body odor strong enough to singe the inside of your nose. This had better be worth it; otherwise I was the biggest fool on the planet. I was hit with a sudden fear that I would step off the bus into a town that was completely unknown—somewhere I'd never been before, like an episode from the *Twilight Zone*.

But back in Nafplio, it was the same as I'd remembered,

and I felt like I was home. People smiled at me, and I even saw some I recognized.

I fell into Thof's arms.

"I can't stand being away from you for two days. How am I ever going to go home?"

"Don't," Thof grinned mischievously.

"Seriously, Thof. You know Pema and I were supposed to head back to Rome the day after tomorrow to catch our flight home. When I told her I wanted to come back to be with you she said she couldn't bear the thought of being with us again. She was adamant about that."

"She'll be fine. She can take care of herself."

"Of course she can, but I feel shitty about it anyway."

"Let me take your mind off of it," Thof suggested, and we fell into bed the moment we got to his apartment.

"Breathe circularly," Thof said, as he traced his finger from my forehead all the way down my front and up my back. "Pull your breath down through the top of your head, down your entire front, and into the perineum. Squeeze there and rock it back and forth to your tailbone, then send it up your spine and out the top of your head."

We did it together a few times until I got the hang of it, gradually moving my energy and breath faster and faster. It was like stepping into another dimension. We came and went from our own bodies into the other's, then completely out of both, toward an ancient divinity. More than once, I caught the scent of animal musk, the dampness of a dog's coat. Day and night blended one into the next. Almost two days passed before we unglued ourselves from one another.

Never could I have imagined that I could feel this way.

"Are you back among us?" Thof smiled. "Come in for landing, Niki."

"I was thinking about a vision I had last week when I was floating in the water." I told him about seeing the hilltop bare of Palamidi, how I traveled alone as a messenger and the family of fox that kept me safe.

"Oh, you vixen! I love you," Thof said. "You have no idea what a relief it is to finally find you again." His eyes brimmed with tears, and I noticed his irises were radiating a yellow light.

"Are they yellow?" he asked me. "Yours are green."

"Yes," I hesitated. Again, he was reading my thoughts. "My eyes aren't green!"

"Yes, they are."

"What are you talking about? My eyes are brown."

"When we make love, or when we're being in love, they turn green. Go look."

"You bet I'll do that," I said with sarcasm. "The things I learn from you."

But I did look, and it was true. The next time I was alone, I looked in the mirror, thought of him, pushed a little energy, and lo and behold, my eyes changed color. They went from dark brown to vibrant hazel. I couldn't believe it.

Forever famished after our ravishing, we headed out to fill ourselves up again. "So tell me more about how your eyes change color."

"It's my spirit guide, my fox," he said. "I can call on him at will now. When he inhabits me all sorts of changes happen. I'm sure you've heard of spirit guides, totems, that kind of thing? You have one too, but don't know it yet."

"What is it? Do you know?"

"Yes, but we'll get into that more later. One thing at a time, Nik."

"Damn it, you always leave me hanging," I teased him. I flashed back on the old woman who rented Pema and me the horrible room when we first arrived in Nafplio. She'd been so angry when we told her we were leaving early, practically spitting, and called Thof a fox.

"But wait, you said all sorts of changes happen. Like what?"

"You'll see."

"Aaarrgg, you are so frustrating!" I laughed and punched him in the arm. Our time was up, though. My flight was the next day and Pema was a no-show.

"I can't leave without Pema! She promised she'd call to let me know what her plans were. I'm going to delay my flight a day in case she missed her connection from Santorini. What if something happened? I'm going to have to call Jin and let him know."

I knew the longer I waited to leave the harder it would be.

"Nik, if delaying your trip makes you feel better, then do it, but I don't think that's the real reason you want to stay."

"No, but it's a reason I can give Jin."

That night, in my usual seat at Koraki, while I nursed my drink, not in the mood for anything and dreading tomorrow, Costa handed me a piece of paper.

"Delivery! I saw this at the post office today and they asked me to give it to you," Costa said.

"Geesh, that's some kind of security system they have going there." I took the folded paper from him.

> N.
> Athens Airport Motel. 10 p.m. tomorrow for
> Rome.
> P.

"Oh my gawd! I can't believe it! Pema is okay! Costa, look!"

He waved a hand at me while heading off to another customer. My mood changed instantly. I wasn't off the hook, but at least she was communicating and maybe didn't hate me entirely. I wouldn't have to go home alone.

...

I took the bus to Athens to meet Pema at the hotel and begin our journey home after two months of traveling. We had to be up by two a.m. to get to the airport by three. The front desk guy told us the airport was so close we should just walk there, given our near penniless state, so in the darkness of early morning we slung our backpacks on for the last time and took a left down the road.

Cars zoomed past, and quickly the quiet road turned into a highway. Drivers honked their horns at us. Ramshackle homes spaced like missing teeth, with long, pitted driveways were set back among the trees along the highway. Dogs tethered to chains leapt out of the darkness, growling and snarling. It was 85 degrees, even this early in the morning. Lorries whizzed by, whipping up small tornadoes of dust and dirt, making us cough and wipe the grit from our faces. We were drenched in sweat and getting nowhere.

"I can't go any further," Pema said.

"Fuck. What the hell was that motel guy thinking? This is insane. We're never going to make it at this rate," I said, the weariness starting to leak out.

"It's so dangerous. This can't be right," Pema said, schlumping her backpack to the ground. "Risking our lives because we spent our last dimes so you could go back to Thof."

"Well, that won't get us to the airport any sooner, will it?" I retorted.

"What a perfect ending to our trip. Seems like a common theme for the last two months," Pema shouted sarcastically over the traffic.

"Why now, Pema? I can't count the number of times you gave me the silent treatment when it came to making tough choices, so I had to make them myself. And now you blame me? Unbelievable! You are so passive-aggressive," I yelled. "This is exactly what you did on the ferry to Greece!"

...

The ferry had been jammed to overflowing; we'd barely made it on board before they lifted the ramp. Making last-minute decisions, standing in long lines to buy tickets, and fighting over whether to reserve a seat or not always left us chasing down our connections. The heat was brutal, the air gelatinous. I squeezed in under a deck to sit in the shade since once again we hadn't gotten a cabin. We'd been buying bread, salami, an apple, and water to last us two days at a time before finally splurging on a full meal in a restaurant.

The thought of the meal we had in Riomaggiore made my mouth water. *Spaghetti alle vongole*! Small clams, so tiny, as small as peas and salty with anchovy paste, mingled with spaghetti in a pond of olive oil. Finely chopped tomatoes and a sprinkling of parsley adorned the dish. The anticipation was orgasmic. We'd had so much fun that night, flirting with the owner, who was old enough to be our father. Only a shower and eight hours of sleep in a real bed could equal the pleasure of a meal.

By midnight every deck chair on the ferry was occupied. There wasn't even a space on the deck, and it was absolutely freezing. The bottled water I'd reserved to brush my teeth with was still hot from the day, so I could use it to warm my hands. It was like being in the desert—brutally hot in the day and freezing at night. I put as many layers on as I could, pulling my clothes out of my backpack.

"Where the hell are we going to sleep?" I asked Pema, not expecting an answer.

"You agreed not to get a cabin!"

"I know! I didn't say I didn't! Geez. You don't need to be so defensive," I said, tearing up. "Look, there's some space on the benches around the pool. Hello? Earth to Pema," I said.

Great, here we go again, I thought. When the going gets rough she gives me the silent treatment. But she followed me, lugging her backpack to the bench. It was covered with dew, and we were freezing.

...

The highway traffic increased now as rush hour started. A driver threw a soda can out their window and it clattered at my feet.

"So now that you're finally voicing your opinion, how about you tell me what we're going to do?"

Pema sunk down onto her backpack and dropped her head into her hands.

"One of us should try to get a taxi while the other stays with the backpacks," she said. "They're too heavy to keep walking with them."

"Right. Let me guess who gets to stay with the bags while I hitch us a ride."

"Listen! We wouldn't even be in this situation if it wasn't for you and Thof! It's all your fault."

I stopped pacing and bit my tongue to keep from crying. "I'm sorry," I said, but she didn't hear me over the din of the traffic.

"We both know who's more likely to get a car to pull over," Pema cried.

I practically threw my backpack at her and stomped off, willing to do just about anything to get away from her. Deep down I knew my anger was a cover for the guilt I felt about my affair with Thof and how it left Pema feeling like a third wheel. Then there was the fear of having to face Jin when I got home.

Up ahead the lights of a gas station shone bright against the dark sky. I had a few coins; I could call Thof. I didn't know what good that would do. In fact, it would waste precious time finding a ride, but I was desperate and at my wits' end.

"Niki!" Thof yelled into the phone over the din of customers and music at Koraki. "What's going on? Are you okay?"

I broke down sobbing at the sound of his voice, the exhaustion and heat coming to full fruition. I'd been holding it at bay, trying to tamp down the emotions and frustrations.

"Pema and I are lost on some highway trying to get to the airport. We're going to miss the plane at this rate. I don't know what to do," I babbled, realizing I sounded like a child.

"Okay, Nik. Calm down. We'll figure this out. Where are you calling from? Is there someone there I can talk to?"

"Hold on." I dropped the phone, leaving it to dangle on

its cord, and went inside. "*Synchoreís, parakaloúme*" I called out to the man behind the counter and pointed to the dangling phone outside. *Sorry, please*. He looked at me with suspicion. Who wouldn't, with my filthy, crying face, but he followed me outside and picked up the phone.

"*Nai. Nai. Acha. Acha.*" *Yes. Yes. Uh-huh. Uh-huh.* Then nothing more I understood. He handed the phone back to me with a pathetic stare.

"Thof," I sniffed.

"Niki, just stay put. Costa is in Athens visiting friends. I'll call him. Hopefully he can be there in twenty minutes. I got the phone number for the station you're at. I'll call back if I can't get ahold of Costa, but I'm sure it'll work out."

Costa was always running off to Athens, visiting friends or buying supplies for the bar.

"I feel like such an idiot. I'm so embarrassed," I said, swallowing back more tears.

"Hang tight, my fox. See you soon. I gotta go now," he said, hanging up the phone.

"Wait! I'm going to the… airport." I ended my sentence to a dial tone. Why would he say "See you soon?"

I'd waited exactly twenty minutes when Costa suddenly appeared, racing into the parking lot, top down, in his yellow Jeep.

"Hop in! Oy, you look like you've been through it," he shouted over the music blaring from his cassette tape deck, the same spooky techno sound they played at Koraki. "Where's Pema?"

"She should be only about ten minutes down the road. She's waiting with our backpacks. I can't believe the rabbit hole that motel guy sent us down. How dumb can you be?"

"Do you mean you or the guy?" Costa jabbed jokingly.

"Ha ha. Well, because of it, I'm sure we'll miss our plane now," I said.

"What the hell happened?" he asked, pulling onto the highway.

"She should be at one of these corners now. Slow down a bit. Damn. It's really hard to tell in the dark."

"You two were walking here? You're lucky nothing worse happened. This is not a good area. Why did you split up?"

"I'm so done with her silent treatments and pouting. It's a long story. We had a big fight, and she was too tired to keep going, so she stayed with the backpacks, and I went to try to find a ride. Honestly, I just needed a break from her. This trip has degenerated into missing buses, sitting on train floors next to stinking, wretched bathrooms for endless hours, and brushing our teeth in the middle of railroad tracks at two in the morning. We argue over when to sleep, where to sleep, what to eat, where to eat, how far to walk before paying for a bus or a taxi. I've had it."

"Sounds about right after spending so much time together."

"She's got to be here. Can you pull over or loop back?"

He pulled into a gravel driveway. I could hear the dogs barking.

"Are you sure it's not further on?" he asked.

"I don't think so. We definitely got as far as the barking dogs. Look! There's my backpack." I jumped out of the Jeep and heaved it into the back. "Could she have taken a ride with someone? What the hell is going on? Why would she dump my pack?" I could feel a pit in my stomach growing. "Can we go back to the motel? Maybe she turned around and went back."

"Good idea."

We reached the motel and checked back in with the front desk guy. Costa asked him if Pema came back.

"*Oxi*," he yawned. *Nope.* "But taxi I call for them say they never show up."

"You called them a taxi? She said you told them to walk," Costa said.

"Yes, walk to intersection. Taxi pick up there." He shrugged, not caring one bit. He could barely stay awake for his shift, much less keep track of two tourists.

"What a nightmare!" I was about to cry again.

"What do you want to do?" Costa asked.

"Do we race to the airport and hope to find her already there or take more time to look for her and lose all hope of making the flight?"

Then it occurred to me that I had a third option: go back to Nafplio… and Thof. I was nearly hallucinating from the heat and no sleep and decided to throw in the towel after one more go-round looking for Pema. Once back in Nafplio, I'd call Jin and tell him I'd missed my flight because of the huge fight Pema and I had; we'd gotten separated, and by then it was too late, and there was nothing I could do. I could figure out what to do about Pema from Nafplio.

An hour and a half later, Costa dropped me off at Thof's apartment, where I fell straight into bed and didn't wake up until noon the next day. By then the telephone bureau for international calls was already closed and no amount of pounding on the door gained me entrance. So the call to Jin would have to wait another day, by which time Pema would be home, I assumed—I prayed. Thof spent the day at work while I swam and lounged, wondering what my plan would be. Jin would be upset, but would get over it, I thought. I'd tell him I was going to hang out in Athens for a few days while waiting for a new flight.

The next morning I walked to the phone bureau and filled out a form with the number and location I was calling and how long I intended to talk. I dropped the form in a box on the agent's desk, took a seat along the wall like a string of others did, and waited for my name to be called. Locals and tourists alike waited for an empty booth in the echoey, high-ceilinged building with whitewashed walls. The light was bright in contrast to the dark, wood-paneled, heavily shellacked phone booths. A single door accordioned open and shut, and a light turned on automatically when you entered the tiny booth.

The man sitting behind the counter called my name and pointed to booth number three. The door clambered shut and all the sound from the lobby was instantly muffled. I felt transported to another time, as though I could watch life go on around me, while mine stood still, safe, silent, and alone. My palms were sweaty as I lifted the receiver. I'd paid for ten minutes and hoped that would be enough. It was expensive. The man who had called my name nodded to me and connected the line. The phone rang. I prayed Jin wouldn't pick up. There was a ten-hour time difference, which made it seven p.m. there. Maybe he wouldn't be home from work yet. Please no, please no, I prayed.

"Hello," Jin's voice on the other end was familiar, jolting me back to reality.

"It's me," I said weakly.

"Niki!" Jin sounded happy to hear me. My throat closed.

"Are you at the airport?" he asked.

"Uh, no. I'm afraid I'm delayed."

"Why? Did something happen? Are you okay?"

"I've lost Pema again."

"What?"

"I'm going to delay my flight a day or so in case she tries to contact me. She promised she would," I explained. "I mean, there's nothing I can do. She's an adult. She can take care of herself, right? But…" I felt my voice wobble and go weak. "I'm in Athens close to the airport…" I had to believe the half-truth myself in order to sound convincing. Something could have actually happened to Pema. I stood up straight in the phone booth and furrowed my brows in concern. They say facial expressions change your chemistry. If you're sad, force a smile and soon you won't be so sad. In other words, fake it till you make it. Now I had to change my tone and energy to make it sound like what I was saying was the whole truth and nothing but the truth.

"What happened, Niki?" Jin asked.

"We came back early from Santo…" I chickened out. I couldn't lie because Pema would tell him the story when she got home. "Hello? Can you hear me? The line is going." I hung up. How shitty of me. Gawd, what had I done? Bought myself a few days, and what good would that do? I felt sick to my stomach over it.

Thof was waiting outside the phone bureau. "Uh-oh, what happened?" he asked.

"Am I such an open book? Geez. I bought myself a day, until I get another flight out, but I didn't tell him anything. I mean, I started to and then I just hung up. My gawd, I suck."

"Listen, get the next flight, face it head-on when you get home, and I'll come see you in a few weeks," Thof said.

"You're right, I have to do that. I can't live with myself otherwise. Wait! What? You'll really come?" Had I heard him right?

"I've been thinking about it. I'll plan a wine promotion tour. I'll convince Dad. Actually, it's perfect timing."

6

At the airline gate in Rome, I asked the attendant to track Pema's name to see if she'd left yet. They didn't have any record of her on any flight, and her ticket was still open. It hit me likea brick—something may have really happened to her and all I'd been thinking of was my own debauchery and how to lie to Jin.

. . .

Pema and I had similar upbringings, but with opposite results. It was what had unknowingly drawn us together when we first met, then kept us together over the years, not to mention being married to brothers and sharing a pitiable mother-in-law. Pema was brought up by an alcoholic mother and an abusive father, I by a narcissistic, adulterous mother and an absent father. Eventually, Pema and her parents rose above it all and became a tight-knit family in spite of her parent's divorce. In fact, Pema and her mother became more like sisters. I didn't know the gory details, but I knew her family life growing up had been bad. But they stuck together through thick and thin. I was envious of her fortitude. I, on the other hand, never got past the bad relationship that festered between my mother and me. Pema came through it an optimist, and I, a pessimist. She had made some tough decisions—to finish college in spite of being pregnant, and marry Bing, even though they both knew it would be disastrous; it had been an inferno from the very beginning.

Pema had real grit. She'd be okay, I told myself.

I found the nearest phone and called Koraki, hoping to catch Thof. Costa picked up.

"Costa, this is Niki. Can you hear me?"

The airline terminal was crowded with Italian families, and names were being called over the speaker system. Each boarding area made its own announcements, competing with the adjacent gate's volume.

"Ah, Niki! Yes! Thof isn't here right now."

"Can you tell him that Pema is still missing? Please give him the message. If he could look out for her."

"Oh, no. Of course! I'll let him know. Are you okay?"

"Shit, they're calling my flight. I have to go. Please tell him."

"Yes, yes. You bet," Costa had a smile in his voice. He always seemed so genuine. I wish I'd spent more time getting to know him.

I hung up without saying goodbye. This took the cake. I really messed things up.

I ordered too many mini scotches during the flight, hoping to calm my flying anxiety and slow my obsessive thoughts of Pema. My mind was racing with all the scenarios that could have happened: she'd met a man and was having the time of her life, she'd been in an accident and was in a remote hospital, she'd been on a bus that was hijacked. No, no, no! I ordered another mini scotch. The stewardess gave me a warning glare this time.

I awoke to an empty seat beside me and wiped away the drool on the side of my mouth. A sour taste coated my teeth. I raised the armrest and stretched my legs across the empty seat, my knees screeching like rusty old cranes. The stewardess gave me the stink eye again. I didn't care; my legs were released now and I couldn't possibly fold them back up.

"We had to find another seat for the passenger seated next to you because your snoring was intolerable, miss," the stewardess informed me.

If that's all it took to get an empty seat next to me, I'd gladly humiliate myself with snoring. I'd have to remember that one.

Jin was at the gate waiting for me, handsome in his pressed black T-shirt, biceps aglow, freshly lotioned.

"What took you so long?" he pressed me.

"We really have some talking to do, Jin."

"I was afraid of that. Where's Pema?" Another question.

"Oh my gawd, I don't know." It was only a half lie this time.

"What do you mean you don't know?"

"I didn't know what to do. She disappeared—" I started.

"Wait, wait. Back up."

"Like I told you when I called, we separated in Santorini. I wanted to go back to Nafplio. She didn't, so I went ahead without her. We'd had enough of each other by then, as you can imagine, together twenty-four/seven. Our paces and rhythms are not exactly the same."

"What did you expect? Wait, you didn't tell me any of this when we talked yesterday. The phone cut out," he reminded me.

"Whatever. She said she might try to get an early flight home and promised to call me to let me know her plans. When she didn't call, I worried that something had happened or maybe we missed each other, so I decided to give her another day. Finally she sent a telegram for me to meet her in Athens at a motel so we could go to the airport together, which I did, but then I lost her again! Then in Rome, the airline said she never used her ticket. Like Thof said… I mean whatI thought was, she's a grown-up; she can take care of herself."

"Who?"

"Pema."

"No, I meant, who said?" Jin asked.

"I said, 'what I thought was…' Forget it. This is getting off to a great start."

"Relax. I have a nice dinner planned for us."

I managed a weak smile. The thought of what was in store for me was depressing, but I thought of Thof and spun some energy from the top of my head down my front and up my spine, imagining he felt it too. I planned to get pretty good at this pushing energy business that he'd taught me. I could swirl it around myself now, clockwise and counter clockwise, feeling the energy pulsing outward, stronger and stronger, as if I could repel someone or move an object across the table.

"You're practically glowing," Jin said.

...

Dinner went off like every other dinner Jin and I had. Nothing honest or meaningful was shared. I glossed over the details of my trip and Jin was content with that. My excuse for not announcing my decision to leave him was exhaustion. His excuse for not asking what I wanted to talk about was avoidance, a plain and simple condition known as head in the sand.

I tried to get back into my work routine. God knows I needed the money. Jin had no idea what the trip had done to my credit card balance. I certainly couldn't ask him to help me out on that one.

I tried to concentrate on work in my studio, but the fax machine chirped and whirred all afternoon with Thof's musings. It started around four, when in Greece it was two a.m., about the time he finished work at the bar. Aside from my studio mate, who was rarely there, I was alone, so I didn't have to worry that the faxes would be discovered. In the three years I'd had the place, Jin had only been there two times for the holiday bashes thrown by our friends down the hall. I loved the space on the top floor of the old brick warehouse and hiked up the seven flights every day. It was between the railroad tracks and a soot-coated overpass in the dark grittiness of the industrial section of town. I'd walk the tracks collecting flotsam and jetsam sprung from the undercarriages of freight cars abandoned by the railroad crews: rusted tie plates, bent spikes, and coiled springs. There were bones, too, from decaying animals left to bleach in the sun—mostly birds and small dogs. I wondered if they'd been hit by a train or wandered off to die. I kept a collection of oddities on the window sill like an altar. They were my talismans, my good-luck charms.

I sat at my drafting table, tapping my pencil and staring out the window, watching the cars zoom across the double-decker bridge that loomed so close to the building. I was desperate to hear Thof's voice, but the time difference and long-distance phone bills were too much, so we had fax sex instead of phone sex. We wrote and wrote and wrote. When I needed a break from all the work I wasn't getting done, I went to the coffee shop up the street and wrote some more. Wrote to Thof, wrote about Thof, wrote to myself about Thof, wrote down the dreams I had about Thof.

My other growing distraction was Pema. As soon as I'd gotten home, I started calling her, but there was never an answer. After three days I decided to try calling her work. On the fourth day I was finally told that she was in, but when the receptionist asked for my name, she told me that Pema wasn't available. It was a great relief knowing she was home and safe, but what the hell had she been doing that week after I'd already gotten home? Where had she been? Why wouldn't she return my calls? And now, Jin was pestering me about what was going on between Pema and me. But as with every conversation, I'd get halfway through explaining and he'd pick up his car magazine or the newspaper or turn the TV on, oblivious that I was even talking.

I weighed the advantages and disadvantages of our relationship all the time. I continued to make lists, a line down the center of the page, pros on one side, cons on the other: handsome husband, money, travel, intelligent, on one side of the line. On the other side: narcissist, no sex, stupid car racing hobby, compulsive liar (or denier). It was a fine line. It always came up nearly even. Maybe that was the best one could expect after five years of marriage, but the debate in my head never stopped.

Back in the studio, Thof's fax arrived announcing his arrival in two weeks! He would do a West Coast promotional tour for his father's wines: San Francisco, LA, Seattle, then Portland, the newest darling of the wine industry. He also announced that he'd be staying in my studio. He insisted. A hotel was apparently out of the question. He wanted to see my life so he could take it back with him. He promised to only show up at night to sleep. No surprise visits. He'd be occupied all day in meetings anyway.

Guilt over Thof's secret arrival, on top of Pema's punitive absence, weighed me down like the dark clouds that delivered the rain seven months out of the year in Portland. I was going to have to show up at her front door and confront her. I couldn't live with it nagging at me anymore and I had to beat Jin to the punch. I decided to show up unannounced when I thought she might be home.

As always, there was no place to park in her neighborhood. I gave in and took a space three blocks away, figuring a short walk would calm me down. I climbed the wooden steps of her rented bungalow and knocked on the screen door. She opened the door without checking to see who was there, as if she was expecting a pizza delivery. When she tried to close the door on me, I blocked it with my foot.

"Pema!" I was stunned at her sunken appearance in the yellow cast of the porch light bulb. "Please let me in. We have to talk. This has got to stop."

The circles under her eyes were more than just from studying late at night. (She was back in school again.) Her skin was ashen, and most shocking was the weight she'd lost. She must have dropped fifteen pounds since I'd seen her only a few weeks earlier in Santorini.

"What's going on? My gawd. Are you sick?" My eyes welled up. I was scared now. Had I set this all in motion?

"Niki, leave. Go."

"I'm not leaving. Why won't you take my calls?"

"Why would you care, Niki? You left me. And now you put me in this triangle between Jin and Bing, keeping your secrets. You think it's easy ducking all their questions? 'Where's Niki?' 'Why are you two not doing things together anymore?' 'Did something happen?' 'Are you guys not talking?' I can't stand it!"

"So you haven't told Bing about Thof and me?"

"No! I haven't told him. I knew that would be your biggest concern. I have enough to deal with. This is all your fault." She was yelling now.

"What's my fault? We agreed to meet so we could fly home together. What happened to you that night? I even stayed longer waiting for you to show up."

"Oh, right. I bet that's why you stayed."

"Pema, I swear it was. I was worried sick about you."

"The night after you left Santorini…" Pema turned and went to the kitchen, grabbed a bottle out of the refrigerator, dug into her purse for a prescription bottle, and washed a pill down with a gulp of water. She stepped back onto the porch and closed the door behind her. "I went back to Tony's… I was too depressed to be alone."

"What happened?"

"I was raped, Niki. Okay? Happy now?" she hissed. "I thought I could deal with it, but after our fight on the way to the airport I couldn't take it anymore. After you went ahead, I stuck my thumb out along that highway and didn't even care what could happen next. I figured if someone murdered me, then fine. I've never been to the bottom like that before in my life. I got the flight to Rome and holed myself up in a room for a week. I had to think it through. Get a grip on myself, decide what to do. Since I've been home, I've thrown myself back into school and work to keep get my life back on track because I'm...." She didn't finish. "Seeing you brings it all back."

"You're what? Oh my gawd, Pema. You're pregnant? Who? Who did it?"

"Roman."

"Roman? Tony's friend? Holy fuck. Oh my God. I'm so sorry. What can I do? I don't know what to say."

"I don't want anything from you. I just need time alone. I can't carry the weight of your secrets around on top of my own. Eventually everyone will find out and stop asking why you and I are no longer joined at the hip."

"But...what did you decide to....?"

"Fuck you. I'll deal with it the way I deal with it. Don't pretend to care now."

"You're my best friend. I do care. I feel so guilty."

"Good. You go and feel guilty. It's all about you after all. It always has been. You don't give a damn about how your actions affect others. Do you even stop to think how Jin would feel if he knew what you did?"

"You know what I've been through with him. I'm done kowtowing to him, dragging him to counseling, begging him to participate in our relationship. Nothing has changed in five years."

"Well then, leave him! Stop the lies and leave! Put your money where your mouth is for once. Leave now! I mean leave my house. Now." She turned on her heels and slammed the door shut on me.

"Call me, Pema. I mean it." I didn't think she heard me.

I sat in my car and sobbed, remembering the night on Thof's boat. The night we'd all met. How innocent it was. It felt like a lifetime ago.

I felt an old familiar panic rising. A desperation. I'd moved on from good friends before—friends who lied or whose personal attacks were over the top. I easily let people drop. But

this time I was the one being dropped. I couldn't afford to lose
another friend. Especially not Pema.

I faxed Thof, recounting Pema's story. His response was not
exactly the compassionate words I was hoping for.

> N.
> Your power, our energy, our souls. Together.
> Don't let Pema distract you. She'll give you
> nothing but drama. Leave her be. Move on.
> I'll be there soon, and the world will be ours
> again.
> T.

It was as if he was afraid Pema would somehow pull me
away from him.

...

In anticipation of Thof's arrival, I tore into a frenzy of
cleaning the studio. I didn't leave a sofa cushion unturned, a
pencil unsharpened, a sill undusted. Even the common bathroom down the hall turned up spotless one day.

"What's gotten into you?" Lisa, my studio mate, asked.

"Oh, I'm just so restless since I got home. Depressed, I
guess. I can't keep my mind on work. Keeping my hands busy
is better than ruminating."

"Yeah, I hear ya. They say it takes twice the time you were
on vacation to get back in the groove of things once you're
back home. So it should be any day for you now."

"Let's hope so."

Ha! If she only knew. As easygoing as she was, I was too
guilty to admit to anyone what I was about to do. What were
the chances that I could pull this one off? My lover sleeping
in my studio, dinners with him every night, and who knows
what else. We were bound to run into people I knew. Who
would I say he was?

...

It was an Indian summer. The best time of year, early October, in Portland. My birthday, too. The leaves were falling, the air was crisp and dry but chilly. What a perfect time to show Thof the city. Maybe we could even run to the coast for a night.

He faxed from his hotel in Seattle with his arrival time. He was taking the train down. So much easier for me, not to have to run out to the airport. The train station was only blocks from the studio. I was practically exploding out of my skin, so nervous I was trembling. I worried that having him here in my world, in my space, wouldn't feel the same as when we were together in Nafplio. Not to mention the stress I felt at the likelihood of being discovered. It added more than a hint of slut into the equation, but I pushed it out of my mind. The extra cup of coffee that morning was really dumb. I should've gone for a run to take the edge off, but somehow I lost track of time. I parked the car at the far end of the lot, out of sight. The sun was almost down.

He stepped off the train into a throng of commuters and picked me out of the crowd without a second of searching, as though he had a sixth sense. We embraced, sending out ripples of energy. People gave us a wide berth, creating a bubble around us as if our energy pushed them all away. It had been like that since the moment we met. Strangers stared at us, mesmerized.

I drove us downtown. It was late enough on a weeknight that hopefully there wouldn't be too many people out. He kept trying to hold my hand as we walked from the parked car to the restaurant.

"Thof, I can't," I shook off his hand and saw the hurt in his eyes. "I'm sorry, but this is my town. You have to remember, I'm married. People will see."

We got a corner table in the back of Pazzo, the Italian restaurant I'd chosen hoping to impress him. I'd never been there, so hoped no one would recognize me.

I ordered *avgolemono*, the lemon soup I'd fallen in love with in Greece. Part of me wanted to relive it, another part wanted to ingratiate myself to Thof—impress him that I'd come to love his culture. I didn't tell him that my stomach was in such a knot it was all I could do to even get a bowl of soup down.

"I love you so much, Niki. You're so beautiful. I even love the way you eat—so little, so slowly. Just a bowl of soup."

"Thof, I wanted to let you know that Pema hasn't talked to Bing or Jin about us."

"How did she get herself in that predicament anyway? No, never mind, I don't want to know."

"She was my best friend! I've lost my best friend over us. Anyway, *predicament*? She was raped, Thof, not locked out of her car."

"Listen, this wine thing is going to be a hit. Everyone is loving it. By the time you're back in Nafplio production will be in full force. I might even have to find someone to take my place at the bar so I can go full-time at the winery." He winked, hinting that it would be me.

"Hold on! I just told you that Pema is in a lot of pain and I've lost my best friend, and you're plotting your business? I need some air." I shoved my chair back and tried not to make a scene weaving through all the other diners. I couldn't believe it. What was I doing with this man? I was on the brink of changing a lot of people's lives and he was utterly insensitive!

"Niki! What's wrong?" Thof followed me outside.

"I'm about to change my life for you… for us… and you are completely insensitive to what that means! Giving up my husband and my best friend who is suffering, not to mention lying to everyone, and you don't even hear me."

"I'm sorry, Niki. I love you. I want us to be together. I'm thinking about our future. This entire trip is going to put us in a very good place. I want to give you everything you could dream of."

"I love you, too. I'm sorry. I've been so stressed out with everything that's happening."

"Let's get out of here," Thof said.

At the studio we made love on the funky old sofa. It served its purpose well. The energy swirled around us like a whirlwind, a tiny twister. It spun so fast it melded us together. Not just skin to skin but soul to soul, hovering above the cushions. I couldn't believe I'd left this behind.

"You've completely possessed me," I said to Thof as he licked my entire body like a dog licks its pup, but teasingly.

He laughed and bit my neck hard. Then again, this time with more skin, muscle, and teeth. I groaned in the dark, fantasizing about his canines. He knew what I was thinking and bit again. The dull pain pleased me.

"You really want it, don't you?" he whispered.

The hair on the back of his neck felt thicker and coarser, his breath musty. An undulation and a sigh were enough to let him know how much I liked it and an invitation for more. In that moment of dark illusion I believed he could. I could not say yes out loud.

He bit again, this time a little lower. "I could you know, but not here," he said touching the inside of my neck with his fingertip. "Not the jugular; that's a myth. It's the carotid that will kill you. Warm, oxygen-rich blood, dark and flowing. You'd drift away. Only four ounces of pressure is needed to kill you." He ran his lips the length of my neck. I pressed him harder against me.

"Float me away," I said.

"Are you ready to die?" he asked. "Will you die with me?"

I didn't answer.

"Are you really ready?" he asked.

"If you bring me back."

"Do you believe that I could?" He was hypnotizing me.

"If you wanted to," I answered him. "It's a risk I'm willing to take." His eyes lifted and I saw the pleasure on his face from knowing that I trusted him to do just that.

"Are you scared of death?" he asked.

"A little," I said after a thoughtful pause.

"Good, I'm glad." He sat up on his knees, his silhouette catching some light from the street. He looked golden and carved and he pulled me up to sit in front of him. "Are there any lights in this place?" He got up to find his clothes.

I clicked on a small desk lamp. I wanted the fantasy to linger, to savor every moment.

"Don't think about dying," he told me, holding me in his arms.

"It's just a game. It's fun," I said. "It's dangerous. I like that."

"I know you do," he said, "but you never know."

"And that's all part of the risk. That's what I like," I said.

"Believe me, I know you do." He laughed his charming, sarcastic laugh.

"The fire you make in me is indescribable."

"Foxes are the fire element. That's us. Fire and fire. You, my dear, steal my fire, galloping away with it to give to others. You're a wise but silly one. I'll always have to keep an eye on you," he said. "You have no idea, but you are a bridge between the gods and the mortals. I'm so lucky to have found you again. We have a long history ahead of us."

"Your eyes are yellow again," I told him.

"My torch for you to see the way."

. . .

I more than needed to have the *D* conversation with Jin. It was practically bursting out of me. I knew he sensed it, yet he easily skated along in a cloud of denial, keeping himself immersed in work. As long as his meals were cooked and his clothes were washed and there wasn't too much fighting, he was as happy as a clam. I didn't know how couples could go along that way for a lifetime. I was always questioning and prodding him, but he didn't want to talk about anything real except work or his car. As long as our issues remained unspoken, all was fine. Keeping face trumped all.

Even at the counselor Jin glossed over our issues. God

knows what he talked about in his own sessions without me. Cars, probably. Or maybe he and the counselor went out for coffee. Whatever it was, we hadn't made any progress in all these years.

"You're late. Where've you been? I've been calling the studio," Jin said as I made a show of throwing my coat off and sighing with exhaustion.

"Sorry, I had the music up really loud to keep myself awake. I must not have heard the phone. You wouldn't believe this fucking client. The changes they're making are killing me."

"Mm-hmm."

"I just want to go to bed. This is going to go on the entire week. Just warning you. 'Night."

"'Night."

Oh, I was good. Where did I get it from? Not even much guilt. Just down to business. *Compartmentalizing* was the word people used. I felt a sudden relief. The rest of the week would be a slam dunk.

And so it was. It went off without a hitch, though with a lot of racing around, hiding in corners, and late nights. The "client" would kill the job come week's end, so I would not have anything to show for it. Of course there would be no money to show for it either.

While Thof was off selling his wine by day, I spent the week writing at the coffee shop and going to the gym. I gave up even trying to get any work done. Evenings we spent eating out and making love. When I got home at night, I showered and dropped into bed in the spare room so I wouldn't wake Jin. But I was starting to feel like a brittle stick, ready to crack. By the end of the week I was relieved to drop Thof back at the train station.

People crowded us on the platform, jostled and elbowed us along with everyone else pushing their way onto the train. I really did love him, but all the sneaking around and scheming and the stress of the week ended his trip on a sour note for me.

He had no clue the circles I'd run to accommodate him.

"I'm sending you a ticket as soon as I get settled back home, my love. The next time we see each other everything will be different. You'll see the moon like you've never seen it before. I have so much more to show you."

"I'm scared, Thof… of everything. Leaving. Staying."

"Move into your power, Niki. Don't be afraid of the dark; it's really the best part. I'm going to show you. I love you! I have to go now. I'll call you when I get to San Francisco."

He grabbed my hand, pressed something into my palm, and closed my fingers into a fist. "Promise not to look until I'm on the train."

"I promise."

The coin from my charm bracelet was inside a piece of folded up paper. It was smoothed down so far, I could barely make out the silver head of the Athena owl inside the outer ring of gold that encircled it. On the folded paper was written:

Float away with me.
Only you know what I mean.
When we meet in the aftermath,
I'll know it's you when our eyes
dissolve to green.

Your lips will brush the coin.
An ancient symbol of trade.
An odd recognition will pass
behind your eyes.

A smell, a taste, a kiss.
But it won't be an illusion.
I got my third wish.

7

I went back to the studio, tidied up, and fell asleep on the sofa the moment my head hit the cushion. I could smell him on it, and it lulled me into a dream. There was a full moon, I was a fox running along the pine scrubs on the rocky slope above the sea. The pups were scampering along behind me, working hard to keep up. It was my job to teach them to hunt and stay alert. I had to be vigilant. Then I became a human dressed in thick furs pummeled by blasts of dense snowfall. One of my pups lost its footing and bounced and slammed its way down the rocks, drowning in the water below, which was simultaneously a vast landscape of snow that stretched into infinity. It made the remaining pups stick even closer to me. I kept them moving. Forward toward the light.

…

"Hey, you, haven't seen you all week. Where've you been? Have you been sleeping here? It seems like you have been." Lisa burst into the studio, chirpy as always.

"Oh, shit. I've been so damned busy."

"Really? Where have you been working? Not here."

"No, this damned client has me in their office all day so

they can look over my shoulder. The only time I've been able to get any creative work done has been here at night. It's been crazy. And now they're killing the job because they made so many idiot changes; the deadline has come and gone. Every-one is fighting. It's an ugly scene. Fuck, how I hate agency work. They're all dick heads. I'm fucking exhausted; lost a week and have nothing to show for it."

I felt like I was starting to drown in my own lies, even believing them myself, surprised of what I was capable of.

...

With the drama gone—on its way back to Greece—my next task was to confront Jin. I had to put my money where my mouth was like Pema said, in spite of my uncertainties about Thof—his strange dark side he seemed to secretly revel in, his line of work which he was so vague about. How well did we even know each other? Regardless, I knew I couldn't go on like this with Jin. I had to conjure my power, like Thof said, and believe I could make it on my own if I had to.

...

Being married to Jin was still a little unbelievable to me. Unbelievable that he was attracted to me to begin with. We'd met in the college weight room. I was doing chin-ups with a twenty-five-pound dumbbell hooked over my crossed ankles while Jin stared in disbelief. I was oblivious. An average look-ing, countrified girl from a small farm town, yet he sought me out. Wooed me until I finally gave in and went on a date with him. I'd only ever known one Chinese person before—Jona-than Chang in middle school—a short, scrawny boy with oily hair and glasses.

Jin and my first date was uneventful, a walk to the local pizza joint, then to the pub for beer and a game of pool. Jin was six-foot-two, muscular, with skin like silk (I found that out much later), had an accent (always a turn-on), and was an intellectual. Eventually, he would introduce me to single malt scotch, teach me Chinese, and take me to foreign movies. I don't think I'd ever seen a movie with subtitles before. He was attentive and generous, not to mention gorgeous. I fell hard for him.

But then we got married.

...

I had to cut the cord now. I picked up the phone and dialed Jin at work.

"Jin, we have to talk tonight. Will you be around?"

"Sure. Dinner?"

"Okay. Call me when you're on your way."

I made my favorite meal—overpriced fresh pasta from the little Italian deli in the neighborhood, and a simple puttanesca sauce I made from scratch.

I'd grown up on canned SpaghettiOs and had never heard the words *pasta* or *prawn*, so when Jin presented me on one of our early dates with *pasta fra diavolo* he'd made himself, I was smitten. For dessert, he even made carrot cake "with real cream cheese frosting," he told me. Years later he confessed that the sauce was from a jar—he'd only added the prawns— and the cake was Entenmann's. When he'd finally admitted it, I brushed it off as charming, that he'd wanted to impress me so badly. For six months of walking on all of our dates, he talked on and on about his RX-7 that was always in the garage. I couldn't wait for him to pick me up in it one day. He even went so far as to tell me that his father didn't approve of him buying a car while still in college. Years later he confessed that there had never been any car! The entire time, he had been baiting the hook to reel me in.

The table was set. I poured myself a glass of wine to take the edge off. Maybe it was the exhaustion from the past week, but the constant dialogue in my head had stopped. No more back and forth. Stay or go? It was as though I turned a light switch off—the relationship had gone dark. I didn't know what would come next, but I knew I couldn't stay in it any longer. The call to adventure was finally stronger than this sham of a marriage.

"I'm sorry, Jin, but I have to tell you something."

Silence came from across the table as though there was a vast tundra between us.

"I met someone in Greece."

More silence.

"I had an affair."

He frowned and put his fork down.

"I had no intention of it happening, but Jin, I've been begging you for sex for years. First, I thought it was all my fault and you let me believe it, even after I discovered your 900 calls. Gawd, it still makes my skin crawl to say those words. I begged you to go to counseling with me. But nothing, Jin. Still nothing. Do you see it? Do you get what I've been through? I'm twenty-five years old and I may as well be a virgin. I'm done."

"Okay."

"Okay? *Okay?* That's it? Are you an automaton now?" I could see the minuscule movements of his jaw clamping and nearly imperceptible squinting of his eyes behind his preppy tortoiseshell glasses. He was a master of containment. It was why he was so successful at his public relations job. I'd never known anyone so emotionless in my entire life. He was locked shut like a vault.

In a rare show of vulnerability, he once admitted to me that he was so scared of his anger turning to violence that he didn't dare crack the door. According to his stories, he'd only opened it two times and both times he said he'd nearly killed someone. I didn't know if I believed him. He'd also told me that he and his brother were in the secret service, and they would always be under surveillance. Fantastical stories that he could give no details about, so why tell me at all except to appear mysterious? When I was a naive twenty-year-old, I admit, I'd fallen for it.

It was as though he had a checklist: hook the girl, marry her, get his citizenship, dismiss the girl. It would take him years, but he was methodical in all his endeavors. I was another one on the list.

"I want a separation," I told him. "I'll find a place."

"No, you stay here, in the house. I'll find a place."

"Why would you do that? I'm the one who cheated."

"Don't worry. I'll go."

And literally, he got up and went, leaving me the entire bottle of red to myself.

...

I faxed Thof about the separation. What time was it there? I had never been good at figuring out the time difference. Would he be sleeping or at work? There was such a small window of time I could catch him at home, between work at the bar and his new wine venture. I'd wait to see what he would say. I wanted him to tell me to come to Greece without any prompting. What if he'd changed his mind? What was the worst-case scenario? I'd find a small apartment here and get serious about work. Serious about a new life. Wasn't that what all my friends were doing? I certainly wouldn't be alone.

Mother always told me, don't get your hopes up, whether for getting accepted into college or landing a job I wanted. Always best to err on the negative side, then you won't be so disappointed when you don't get what you want. I'd been fighting the cynicism all my life.

According to her, I was in for hard work and sacrifice. Life was not meant to be enjoyed but suffered. "Too good to be true" was always lurking in my thoughts, undermining so many things. My husband was too good looking, made too much money, our modern house in the hills was too nice. All too good to be true. It dawned on me that maybe my mother was jealous of me.

I could handle the change to a simple middle-class life in a sunny Greek coastal village. I didn't mind hard work, but was not beyond some hedonistic pleasures in life. Mother hadn't succeeded at stomping out all of life's joys.

At two in the morning, Thof's response came whirring through the fax machine: PACK YOUR BAGS!

Two days later he picked me up at the airport in Athens.

8

The only thing that is constant is change.

— Heraclitus, 500 BC

Of course, we spent a week in bed. My hip was out from all the flexion, and I was losing weight again in spite of all the eating we did when we finally uncoiled, showered, and made our way into town.

After a glorious week, life, work, and bills piled up and we were spit out into the real world again. Over lunch we talked about my new position at Koraki. I wanted to work and tuck away some money, and Thof needed someone to cover for him so he could concentrate on growing Ugo's wine business.

"This is all so perfect, Niki. This is really going to give me a chance to put my father's name on the map."

"You certainly attract a crowd at the bar. You obviously know what you're doing."

"By the seat of my pants. Good food, good music, a smile, and people will come. But now I want to help my dad make a mark."

"Seems like he's already done that, hasn't he?"

"Yes, but my cousins are in charge of the new shop. They do the heavy lifting, so to speak. Dad enjoys his days sitting out front talking to friends and customers. Now that I'm back, though, I have to make up for lost time."

"What do you mean lost time? Your dad doesn't approve of you? There's so much about you I don't know, but I feel I've known you forever."

"We have known each other forever. You're finally getting it," he said. "Anyway, I think Dad approves of me now. It took me forever to finish college. I was lost and felt my soul fracturing. I didn't realize it at the time, but I was mourning my mom and then I started experimenting with drugs. I really messed up. I still feel badly about it. It should have been me cutting the opening ribbon to the new shop, but Dad recruited my cousins instead. So I'm motivated to build some margins fast for him. It suits me more than ouzo anyway. I don't even like it. I already have some pretty solid relationships with grape growers and some leads for distributors. Dad was skeptical when I told him I wanted to take it to the U.S. and Asia, but he realizes now I was right. So, Niki, if you can be patient while I fly off to the ends of the earth, I think you'll see that it'll be worth it."

"Absence makes the heart grow fonder." I didn't add "for somebody else"—yet another of my mother's charming tropes. It was a constant battle fighting her voice in my head. Even after she died, the voices wouldn't shut up. "You prove yourself to your dad and I'll prove myself to you." I said to Thof.

"You already have. Just do it for yourself and have fun. And you won't have to worry about the books. That's the one thing I'll leave for Dad to do. You won't have to worry about a thing."

"I'll take you up on that. Numbers aren't my strong suit."

Stay away from the bills? Again? Don't go there Niki, I told myself.

Our lovemaking that night verged on carnivorous. I wondered if he was putting on a bit of a show for me with his licking and nuzzling. The out-of-body experiences were incredible, but I wondered how much of the hallucinatory feelings were from the heat and so much sweating. I'd never sweated so much in my life. No spin class or boxing workout at the gym came close to this intensity. The stamina expended and acrobatics performed bordered on circusy. I let it drift to the back of my consciousness, and before I fell asleep, I found my Athena coin and slipped it onto Thof's key chain.

...

With Thof off on his first trip, I was excited to start my new adventure working at the bar. I'd spent the winter hanging out there, getting to know the locals, and observing Thof and Costa work seamlessly together. I felt like I could practically run the place myself if I had to, right down to the fake smile and sarcasm I knew Thof used when certain customers got under his skin. I was glad to be so busy that I barely had time to miss him.

I learned the nuances of how to pour wine and memorized the ingredients for assembling all the menu items. I'd eaten enough of them; that was for sure. Costa taught me how to pull espresso shots. I even knew the closing routines. I'd been through it so many times, helping Thof, so we could get out of there early.

It was only the mundane things I didn't know how to do, like how to use the cash register and Thof's antiquated way of taking orders, using old-timey carbon copy pads. It was charming but not practical. And I worried about being able to cut off drunk customers. He had such a subtle touch, always able to steer them out the door without incident. No one ever picked a fight or bullied him. Of course he was six foot two. I didn't think I had the confidence to pull that off. I looked like a pushover, an easy target in my high heels and platforms. I was no bruiser.

Now that spring was right around the corner, it meant that small injections of tourists would be trickling into town, business would soon pick up, and the locals would get back to the demands of visitors. It also meant hillsides exploding with the fresh green color of spring grasses, being able to get back into the glorious sea, and lingering aromas of wild herbs. By August, the landscape would be parched brown, the sea swarming with foreigners, and the locals wishing to never see another tourist again. But now, I was ready to step up to managing the bar. It ended up being way more work than I ever imagined. If it wasn't for Costa sharing the load, I wouldn't have had a minute to myself. Thank gawd I didn't have to do the books on top of it all, but I did want to know that the margins were good with the changes I'd made. Thof told me if anything was ever a concern, he would let me know. He seemed to trust me implicitly and never told me to change anything I'd done. There appeared to be an endless flow of money coming into the bar. Whatever idea I came up with, it was implemented: more international wines, more expensive ingredients. Whatever gadget I wanted, I bought: a fancy convection oven, a commercial espresso machine. Costa said it had always seemed to be that way even before I got there. It wasn't his business to pry. He just had fun with it.

"Honestly," Costa told me one afternoon, "I think the old man is loaded and he's keeping the bar in the black to keep Thof occupied."

"Why would he have to do that?"

"Well, Thof doesn't have the best record for sticking to one thing or staying out of trouble."

"Really? I'm surprised. He seems so focused."

"Sure he is now, but in college… we were all pretty worried about him… like mother, like son, if you know what I mean."

"Oh, shit," I said, remembering what Thof had told me about his mother's episodes.

"It's not really for me to say. I shouldn't have brought it up. I'm sorry; I don't mean to worry you. He's been great for the last few years—healthy, on track, determined to make this wine business of his dad's work."

"Geez, it sounds pretty serious."

"Yeah, well, if you don't mind… uh… don't let on that I said anything."

"You got it." I made a mental note to ask Thof when he returned about his days of wanderlust. I could count on Costa to throw me enough clues to point me in the right direction.

9

"Let's go up to the rocks. It's been ages," I suggested to Thof the night he finally got back after being gone for four weeks. It was our safe place. The place it all began. The place I could most likely get him to reveal more about himself.

"Are you feeling okay about me working at the bar?" I asked.

"Sure, why?"

"Oh, just checking in. I'm curious how I'm doing with the bottom line."

"You're doing great. You're a natural. I love your bottom line."

"Ha ha. Okay, I'll take your word for it. What was it like for you when you first opened it?"

"I saw how my dad ran his store, but a bottle shop is a different beast than Koraki. The bar is a restaurant, a music venue, and most importantly, the heartbeat of the town. I never imagined the impact it would have on the lives of everyone here. And then there are the tourists. Yet another beast to contend with."

"It's amazing what you've done. What'd you do before the bar?"

"Kind of ashamed to say nothing worthwhile. I ran around a lot, did some crazy shit, took too many drugs."

"You obviously grew out of that." I massaged around his vulnerability like you would around a bruise.

"I guess I scared myself. I got to a point where I had to make a decision—live half out of my mind with all the voices in my head and probably end up dead or try one more time to close the door on that part of myself and come back into the fold of normal people." He made air quotes around the word *normal*. "Contain myself in a lower dimension. Plus, my dad was really hurting. I finally could see it."

"Sounds like more than just college antics."

"The people I hung out with were so tripped out of their heads that they accepted me without question. For the first time ever I felt like I could be who I really was. Who I am."

"What do you mean, who you really are?"

"I've never told anyone what I'm about to tell you," Thof said.

"Go ahead. Is something wrong?"

"Well, some people might say that. I consider it a gift."

"You consider what a gift?"

"You're going to think I'm nuts."

"Try me."

"Well, hmm. I don't know how to say this."

"Just say it then."

"I'm a therianthrope."

"Wait… a what?"

"I don't know the word in English. I'm connected to a fox. I'm one with him."

"A fox? You're really serious, aren't you?"

"I'm not saying I turn into some crazy monster when there's a full moon. It's more like a past-life experience coming back to me. It's an intense spiritual takeover."

"I believe in past lives, but… you turn into a fox?"

"Most people think of wolves, but that's just in the movies. You can connect with any animal."

"A werefox?"

"That's the word! You're catching on. But seriously, I get

depressed sometimes, and he comes to me then and takes me off with him. It's the way I cope with the darkness I fall into when the depression comes. And, I have to admit, it does happen mostly during full moons."

I flashed back to the first night he brought me up here to the rocks overlooking the water. I'd had the strangest vision earlier that day, and later the dream of being a fox with my cubs.

"I'm getting goose bumps," I said.

"I don't mean to scare you."

"No, I'm not scared. In fact you won't believe me now," I said.

"Yes, I will. You saw it didn't you?" Thof asked.

"The fox," I said. "Yes. That first night you brought me here. You were right about feeling like I'd been here before. Then I had the strangest dream. So many things exist that we have no understanding of, on multiple dimensions even." I couldn't believe this was happening, couldn't believe how easily accepting I was of his story. I could never tell anyone. They'd think I was nuts.

"I think I've been able to see the dark side since I was a kid," I told him. "Or maybe I wanted to and manifested it. I've never admitted that to anyone either."

"People think darkness is evil or scary. I think we've lost our connection to it, to the monthly cycles, to Gaia, the moon."

What could I say? I'd felt it. There was no denying. But it was crazy. Was he crazy? I wondered if he'd dealt with the possibility that he'd inherited his mother's mental illness. Did his drug use bring on the shape-shifting episodes he claimed to have, or did he use drugs when he felt one coming on in order to numb himself from it? I wondered which came first.

"Now I can maintain a day-to-day life and keep all that at bay. Without the drugs I've been able to see the value in life—Dad, Costa, and now you. If it means closing that one door so three others open, then it's worth it. And now that I have you, we can crack that door open together, my little fox." He petted my head. "You're getting your period, aren't you?"

"Any minute now." My mind was doing flip-flops. I didn't know if I should be worried about what he'd told me or embrace it. I prayed that I didn't leave my old life for a madman.

"I want you. I miss your blood."

We dashed back to our den on the rooftop of Thof's apartment.

"You'll only bleed for a day now. It'll be light. I got almost all of it," he told me.

"You blow my mind." I couldn't explain it, but in fact my period was only one light day. It was always that way when we were together. One day was fine by me. When he was traveling, it lasted four days or more.

We easily settled into the flow of things when he returned from his trips. He'd keep me company at the bar, like I used to do with him when we first met—telling me stories of his travels and new wine customers. Costa would close so Thof and I could get a brandy at a cafe on the harbor and watch the tourists or we'd make love on the rocks above the beach before walking home. I couldn't believe I'd been here for over a year now. It seemed like yesterday that I'd arrived. I was amazed how far we'd come in a year. How far, literally, I'd come—six thousand miles, ninety-nine longitudes.

...

Sliding into my second winter in Nafplio, Costa and I worked seamlessly together. The off-season brought few tourists and an entirely different vibe filled the town. With more free time on their hands, locals filled the bar. It was a much more relaxed atmosphere, even when Koraki was packed. When Costa and I were both behind the bar we floated around each other as though on ice skates. It was a tight space, no room for tripping up, especially when we were moving so fast. We communicated with a nod, tipping each other off about who to keep an eye on, who was ready to pay, or who had been waiting to order. We became known for tossing things across the room at each other. We were both ambidextrous and would throw with one hand while catching with the other. Towels, corkscrews, and saltshakers would go flying over the customers' heads. Most didn't even notice until it had already whooshed by. They loved the show. The few out-of-towners who didn't know us thought we were a couple, the way we laughed and casually touched each other. Impossible to pass each other behind the bar without body contact, it was like eight-hour shifts of foreplay. I couldn't deny that I hadn't thought about it and felt a twinge of longing. After a particularly busy night at the bar, Thof gone for what seemed like weeks, Costa offered to drive me home. We leaned against his Jeep taking in the fresh air, brilliant stars, and quiet calm, talking about the crazy customers that night. We laughed over conversations we'd overheard and secret gropes we'd seen under tables.

We had nicknames for the more eccentric regulars: Jesus, the bearded laundry man who dressed in flowing robes and always seemed to sneak up on you; Magnificent Sperm Man, the seventy-two-year-old man who told me one night that his doctor declared him the most robust senior he'd ever seen, after which he went home and immediately jerked off to his shirtless self in the mirror; the Beaver, who whispered into my ear one busy night (his wife patiently waiting for him by the door) that he wanted to gnaw the jeans off my ass (I wanted to gag); Porn Woman, who lifted her shirt every time she sat at the crowded bar to show off her triple D implants to anyone who wanted to gawk. It gave us hours of bent-over-laughing episodes talking about them all.

"Oh my gawd, did you see who Mr. Kim was with tonight?" Costa asked. "The woman with the poofy hair?"

"Yes! That was his wife's sister. They were practically necking. Then he passed food out from his store again to everyone sitting at the bar. That rotten chicken yakitori he tries to pawn off on everyone. I had to tell him to stop."

"Is that like the third time he's tried that?"

"At least. That's when he fell off his stool—when they got up to leave. He kept saying, 'No cost to you! No cost to you!'"

"Here's to the newly anointed Mr. No Cost to You," Costa mimicked Mr. Kim and we burst into a new round of laughter.

I lifted my head from his shoulder and turned to face him. He stopped talking. I felt the cool air on my face as he kissed me on the lips, so casually, as if second nature.

"Hey, what's that about?" I tried to step aside, but he gathered me up in his arms and pressed me against the car.

"No cost to you." He smiled, and I relented. We made out until my chin was red and stinging from his bristly cheeks and the air turned chilly. When an occasional car drove past, we ducked down, laughing, hiding from their lights. "I've been holding back that kiss for weeks," Costa confessed.

In such a tiny town it was inevitable that people hooked up, then got caught. I'd never understood why people were so careless, living with the sideways glances and whispers. But now, in an instant, I understood. All reason went out the door. It was like we were in a bubble, invisible, when in fact it was the opposite. A light was cast on us. The best defense was to hide in broad daylight. We palled around town like best friends. People were perplexed, and the gossip grew. When Thof was home the three of us would go out together to catch up on business.

How could I be living this lie? With Costa it felt like we were kids experimenting, laughing and goofing off. We both knew it wasn't serious, much less sustainable. I told myself it was harmless, a fleeting diversion when Thof was gone for weeks at a time. But this made me as bad as Jin's father. Even worse, I was repeating the lustful offenses of my own mother, who had cheated on my father right under his nose. Was it genetic?

$$10$$

"Nik…I wanted to hea…ur voice." Thof's phone connection was shaky at best.

"Thof, I can hardly hear you. You're cutting out. Are you okay? It's two in the morning. I thought you were in Korea." It sounded like chaos in the background, a crowd of voices shouting and the sound of banging doors. I couldn't make out what language was being spoken.

"I'm delayed… in Turk…custom… only one pho…ca…" Thof was shouting into the phone to be heard above the din.

"For how long? What happened?" I was shouting now too.

"Wine shipmen…." Suddenly the shouting on Thof's end got even louder, as though someone was yelling directly at him, and the line disconnected with a grating crunch.

This had happened before. He had the worst luck at customs. They often delayed him getting home. I knew there was nothing to worry about, but still, there was no way I'd get back to sleep after that.

I got up and made coffee, paced around the apartment, and asked Minky, Thof's cat, what she thought could have happened to Thof this time. She stared at me bleary-eyed in the sudden light, happy to have company in her nocturnal restlessness. This was going to be a long day full of worry on top of the aggravation of trying to fix some problems at Koraki that had popped up.

Ugo was at his usual post, sitting on a flimsy wooden chair outside his shop door. Above him, a small, hand-painted sign, newly distressed to look old, hung beneath a lantern. White marble slabs framed the faded chalky-blue double doors of the entrance. The stoop was littered with specks of white-wash that was flaking off the building. The second story was shuttered with decaying wooden slats. It was as if the place was dying from the top down.

He wore a white tank top tucked into black slacks, cinched and gathered high around his potbelly with a brown belt. His well-worn but clean leather huaraches had seen many trips to the cobbler. His stomach preceded him as he smiled at the tourists and shouted hellos to his friends. When he saw me approaching his face dropped.

"*Yiasou*," I greeted him, businesslike. He thrust his chin at me and headed inside the shop. Don't overdo it, I thought, rolling my eyes at his back and skinny hunched shoulders as I followed him.

The shop was furnished with heavy chairs and tables, making it feel more like a funeral home than a liquor shop. Dark still-life paintings of fruit hung on the walls alongside plaques inscribed with nonsensical Greek platitudes: *The many words are poor, Slowly the vegetables, Catch the egg and mow it.*

An antique cash register sat heavily on display on a chunky table. Next to it a dimpled brass bucket held dried fern fronds that exhaled a perpetual ring of dust onto the tabletop. Even the air seemed yellowed and jaundiced.

"Have you heard from Thof? He called at three in the morning and sounded like he was being delayed at customs again, but the connection was so bad I didn't get any details."

"*Oxi*." *No.*

Okey dokey. The man was a gem.

"Will you let me know if you hear from him? In the meantime, I'm sure you know that the exhaust system has to be replaced at Koraki. I've delayed it waiting for Thof to pay the contractors but now he's unreachable. He said you do the books, so I need to ask you for the money so I can get this done before the inspectors come back."

"What books?" Ugo asked.

Maybe we weren't understanding each other. Again. I thought my Greek was pretty good. I had a knack for languages, not to mention my own private tutor. Ugo was a mumbler, and I was certain he pretended not to understand my English, much less my Greek. He engaged with tourists every day in his shop. He clearly understood them.

"I'm knowing nothing about Koraki's books," he muttered.

"But Thof told me you take care of them."

"You must be mistaken. I've never done the bar's books. Thof has always insisted on doing them himself—keeps them from me, in fact."

I pretended to brush it off and wondered what was behind the lie. But I was jumping to conclusions, right? After everything he'd told me about his past, why would Thof lie about something as simple as this? Ugo was right; it was probably a misunderstanding. Or was he lying too? I had to stop with the fantasies and proceed with the repairs, cash or no cash. Everyone knew Thof was good for the money. It was why vendors had been so forgiving lately when their invoices didn't get paid for sixty days or more. I had to talk to Thof about that.

I ordered a new exhaust system on credit and told the contractors to remove the old one and install the new one. Days went by and nothing got done. The workers didn't show up until late in the afternoons, obviously hungover, smoking and laughing. No amount of cajoling or promise of bonuses made a difference. It was as though they were spiting me. Finally I threw in the towel.

I left a note with Ugo telling him I had urgent business in Athens and begged him to handle the workers. He would be furious, but secretly gloat, taking credit for getting the job done.

He'd snap his fingers and the workers would finish the job. He knew I'd been struggling for days with them. It was as though he was waiting for me to fail.

"Costa, come to Athens with me," I implored. "Koraki is closed. What else do you have to do? We need a vacation."

"You just assume I have nothing to do if the bar is closed? I do have a life, ya know," he said, laughing.

"All right. Think of it as a mandatory meeting. A work retreat to regroup and brainstorm some new ideas for the bar. All expenses paid!" I said, with no intention of doing anything but reading a trashy novel and lying on a beach.

"On one condition," Costa said. "We go to Cesme instead. Athens will be no vacation—all sweaty and grimy, teeming with Americans."

"Yes, that is a horrible thing," I teased him.

"I'll introduce you to some old friends and we'll go to the hot springs, then we can hit some resorts."

...

I couldn't believe I'd done it. Leaving the repairs with Ugo and closing the bar for another week was one thing; hitching a tin can with wings to fly off to Turkey with Costa was another. People did it all the time I told myself—run off with a lover and fly in these rattling buckets. I said a prayer and white-knuckled Costa's hand all the way.

"We'll get you a pill for the flight back," he assured me.

I'd never been to Turkey before. Costa knew the beach town well, since he'd gone often as a teenager. Unlike Nafplio, the beach was sandy, not rocky, and the buildings Ottoman, with pointy towers and bleached facades. It was a relief to let Costa lead the way. He even spoke a bit of Turkish. My only judgment was that for his entire life, he'd never ventured further than an hour away from Nafplio. It sounded elitist, but I couldn't help it. I'd also grown up isolated in a tiny town, but I'd traveled all my life and left home by the time I was seventeen. Costa had hardly left Nafplio, nestled in a deep inlet on the Peloponnese Peninsula, directly west of the overrun islands of Greece and the coast of Turkey's resort beaches. Unlike me, family and community were in his bones. He would stay in Nafplio until he died.

Growing up, my own aunts and uncles were practically strangers to me. I'd never realized how much until coming here and meeting Thof and his friends. Their tight community gave them a confidence I'd never had. They had an invisible safety net that they all seemed to take for granted, gossiping constantly about each other, complaining and making fun of their neighbors and relatives, yet they were close-knit and held together like a patchwork quilt. I envied that, but would never give up my carefree lifestyle, even though sometimes it felt like there was a hole in me, like I was hollow. I didn't want to live under the expectations of relatives. My cousins asked my mother why I wasn't at the family reunions. Did I need money to fly home? It was constant pressure, like being asked when the babies would come. How dare they? Ultimately it was my mother who was ashamed that I was the only cousin never there, as though it was a reflection on her. As though I was too good for them all.

Everyone we encountered embraced Costa like they were long lost friends. He was the most positive, upbeat man I'd ever met. He had no time for self-indulgence and his attitude was contagious. I'd never laughed as much as I did with him. Such a change from Thof. Not that Thof didn't have a sense of humor, but it was overshadowed by his intensity and dark moods. I was attracted to these two very opposite men. Opposites who were also best friends.

We agreed on a beach club tucked in a lagoon of turquoise water. Normally the place would have been crawling with bikinis and brawn, but it was early season, and we had the place virtually to ourselves. We ordered *mezze* and *raki*, traditional small plates and a powerful anise brandy, from the outdoor bar and headed down the path to a secluded palapa. Dried brown palm fronds hung over a bamboo frame like bangs and rustled softly in the breeze. Longer clumps were tied to the corner posts in ponytails. As the sun was setting over the Aegean Sea, we waded knee-deep out into the water and hoisted ourselves up onto a wide bleached hammock.

Tethered to two weathered pilings, it swayed an inch above the water. Soon the locals would wake up from their siestas and sprinkle out onto the beach and narrow streets, reclaiming them from the tumult of tourists finally gone home. A hustle-bustle of families would vie for seats at the beachside cafes, each with its own music blasting out of its doors, competing happily with its neighbor's. The high-pitched whine of Vespas filled the streets with glee.

Costa and I never stopped talking and the topic of work never came up. It was so natural being with him and the sex was perfectly wonderful, too; relaxed and easygoing. Satiated with food and talk, back in the palapa, we dropped into bed early, made love and fell asleep to the phantom swaying of the hammock.

I tried to justify my recklessness and wondered if Thof wasn't having trysts along the way, too. I didn't believe he would, but part of me almost hoped he did so we would be equal in our wantonness. He was gone more than he was home this last year. What did he expect? I woke in the morning in the same position I'd fallen asleep in.

...

We had planned a full day of lying on the beach, drinking margaritas and people watching. Maybe we'd hook up with some of Costa's old friends for dinner or music. But first things first—breakfast. We found a table at the Angora Resort overlooking the harbor.

"See the guy at three o'clock, the one with the hat and Hawaiian shirt?" I started my favorite game of making up names for strangers the same way we made up names for our customers. "I'd guess his name is Mr. Schnauzenhoser."

"Mr. Schnauzenhoser, sir, please do introduce me to your wife, such a lovely penguin she is," Costa puckered his lips and spoke with an affected accent. "Oh, it's Mrs. Fattinround, is it? So pleased to make your acquaintance. I am Sir Bugger Abit."

We burst out laughing. Costa was a natural at the game. I didn't even have to explain myself when I launched into it the very first time. Sometimes we'd laugh so hard we'd snort up our drinks and had to leave the room to recover. It was such a cathartic release. I could feel my shoulders drop down an inch. Thof always scolded me for making fun of other people. I argued that there was no harm; it was just a game. It's not like they knew we were making fun of them.

"Niki," Costa said, reaching across the table to take my hand, gazing into my eyes, suddenly serious. "I love you. Stop what you're doing with Thof and be with me. There, I finally said it."

My mouth dropped open. "Oh fuck, oh fuck, oh fuck," I hissed behind my napkin.

"That wasn't the response I was expecting." Costa scanned the room of breakfast eaters in the direction I was looking.

"Oh, fuck! What the hell is he doing here?"

There was Thof, entering the restaurant in a camel-colored linen jacket with a Nehru collar, wearing only a gold chain underneath it, perfectly pressed jeans, and brand-new huaraches. I'd never seen anyone who could pull off such a perfect combination of suit with no socks, except in the *New York Times* men's fashion magazine.

"Stay calm. Relax," I whispered to Costa. "Shit, he's coming this way." I took an extra-long exhale out of my mouth like I'd learned to do in yoga.

Thof scanned the room as he seemingly floated into the restaurant—man of the world, *Wall Street Journal* tucked under his arm. He glanced at his Cartier watch, obviously on his way to meet someone. Then he found us.

"Niki? Costa?" For a split second his face fell, a crack in the veneer.

"Thof?" Costa and I said at exactly the same time.

"What are you doing here?"

This time all three of us blurted at the same time. "I…" "We…" Again we all started talking at once.

"I thought you were on your way to Korea," I finally wedged in.

"There was a last-minute change, and then a delay, like I tried to tell you on the phone. I got the call at the airport as I was about to board. There's a potentially huge opportunity here so I took a bucket flight over since I was so close. I'm catching the Korean flight this afternoon, in fact." Thof explained. "And you two? What's going on?"

"You wouldn't believe the week I've… we've had. I tried to get ahold of you. I left so many messages with the concierge." I paused, waiting for Thof to fill in why he hadn't returned my calls, hoping whatever reason he'd give would steer the conversation away from Costa and me. But he stood silent, waiting. Costa picked up where I left off.

"The main exhaust over the stove broke down. It happened to be the same day the inspectors made their surprise visit. It could not have been worse timing. They shut us down on the spot." I was surprised to hear Costa stretching the truth.

I jumped in. "I needed cash fast to get the repairs going. When I couldn't get ahold of you, I went to Ugo. Well, you can guess how that went over. I don't know what that man has against me. Oh, and remind me next time you're home there's something I need to ask you concerning the books."

"So what are you two doing here?" The lines between Thof's brows were deepening.

"I'm trying to tell you," I said. "Between your father, the workers not doing a damned thing and… everything, I convinced Costa to get away for the weekend. He agreed we both needed a break and his friends happened to invite us to their house."

"Then why are you here?"

"We had business to discuss and didn't want the distraction of his friends, much less bore them with our talk. We're just having breakfast, Thof." I gestured to my pad of paper and pen. Thank gawd I'd brought it along. I'd gotten into the habit of always having paper and pen to jot down my thoughts, work out my frustrations, and sometimes sketch. There were a few arrows on the page heading off in different directions. Thof knew the game. Arrows pointing toward the person I was targeting with my mocking words.

"I hope your 'huge opportunity' was worth the detour and the detainment." I tried to get out from under the interrogation spotlight.

"Listen, I'm meeting him here now. He's taking me out to see his vineyard. Just a short drive. I have to be at the airport in four hours. I'm sorry I can't catch up with you now." He spoke to me only, clearly avoiding Costa's gaze altogether. "I love you, Niki. See you as soon as I'm back." He pulled the coin out of his breast pocket and touched it to his lips.

"I love you too." He leaned over and kissed me on the lips. I felt a buzz that he pushed through me, and his eyes sunk into mine.

"I remember," I said, hypnotized.

Thof smiled and walked away, ignoring Costa.

"You remember what?" Costa asked.

"Oh… nothing… just an inside joke." I tried to brush it off, but felt sick to my stomach. How could I have thought this was a good idea?

"Jesus, do you think we were convincing?" Costa asked.

"I don't ever want to be in this position again, Costa," I snapped, trembling and trying to hold back the tears.

His happy-go-lucky mien fell flat for the first time.

"It's not like I planned this," he said. "It's shitty. The whole thing is shitty. I feel like a real piece of shit. Shitty shitty bang bang," he desperately joked, failing to even convince himself of it.

"I can't believe you can be so callous, Costa. We're liars."

"What's done is done. Let's please try to enjoy the time we have left," he said, covering up his hurt. "Niki, this isn't another fling. I promise you. You deserve better than Thof. Trust me."

"Why would you say that? I love him. Other than being gone too much, he's showered me with his love and attention. He cracked me open and showed me that I can have joy again. And this is how I repay him. I am a liar and I'm ashamed of it."

"There are things you don't know about him, Niki."

"There are always things you don't know about your partner. Discovering them along the way is what keeps a relationship going—keeps it from being stale. Hopefully the learning never ends."

"I'm talking about things you don't want to know, Nik. I didn't want to tell you…"

I picked up my pad of paper and pencil and left without saying a word or looking back at him. I deserved everything that was coming to me.

11

We cut the trip short and returned to Nafplio the next morning, silently going in opposite directions—Costa to his apartment and me to work. I needed some space and wished the spinning thoughts in my head would stop. Costa had been about to tell me something about Thof before I walked out on him.

At the bar I found Ugo lingering in the street out front. He had a large envelope in his hand and a suspiciously raised eyebrow. He handed the envelope to me and waved a hand at the bar indicating both Look what I did for you, and You never could have done it alone; a man must be in charge. In this case, he was right. He put his hands together in prayer position and bowed ever so slightly at me.

"*Efaristo,*" I said to him with a half-smile. *Thank you.* I could not figure this man out for the life of me.

Jin didn't need an address; the envelope was marked simply, Niki Sho, Nafplio, Greece. That's how small the town was. Pema must have told him that was all he'd need to get it delivered to me. Divorce papers struck me like a slap across the face. Jin had been such a shell for so many years it was no surprise that I hadn't given him a second thought since arriving in Nafplio over a year ago, but divorce was still a mark of failure.

A note in his handwriting was clipped to the papers.

> Niki,
>
> I met with a lawyer and drew up the details, put the house on the market, will look for job somewhere else, maybe back east. Given the circumstances of your fleeing, I kept as much of the proceeds from the house as legally possible. You're on your own now.
>
> J

Nice. I threw the envelope on the stack of mail on the bar that had accumulated while we were in Turkey. The dust had settled, literally, while I was gone. There was a thick layer covering everything, but the new exhaust system hummed.

I picked up another envelope from the stack. It was from the bank. It had been mistakenly delivered to the bar instead of to Ugo's shop, where Thof had the business mail delivered. I ripped it open and scanned down the page, trying to decipher what I saw. There was the withdrawal for the exhaust system work—quite a chunk of change—but compared to the balance posted at the bottom of the page, it was a drop in the bucket. Where were the nightly deposits from the bar? Deposits were posted, but not in the amounts that I'd counted every night—around $1000 a night. The sums listed on the statement had an extra zero—$10,000 a night.

"What's wrong? Looks like you've seen a ghost." Costa came into the bar. "Whoa, look at that shiny mother." He pointed to the new exhaust. "You tested it?"

"Uh, yeah," I said sheepishly, suspicious of his good mood. I wondered which one of us would be more upset with the other—him for being turned down, or me for getting us into the situation of being found out.

Costa flipped the switch a few times, starting and stopping

the deep whirring hum of the fan.

"Would you stop that, please?" I stood at the bar, staring at the paper in my hand. "The mail today has been quite auspicious," I told Costa.

"What do you mean? Why?"

"Well, first of all, Ugo delivered my divorce papers."

"What? Ugo? How could he possibly deliver divorce papers?"

"The envelope was simply addressed with my name and Nafplio. While we were gone, the mailman gave it to Ugo, who was kind enough to hand deliver it this morning when he saw me come in. You should've seen the look on his face. If I didn't know better, I'd bet he steamed it open."

"Oh shit, Niki. I'm sorry."

"No, no; it's okay. What could I have expected? I'm good at sticking my head in the sand. It was inevitable."

"Then there's this." I showed him the statement in my hand. "I have a lot of experience finding shocking news in the contents of utility bills and bank statements. One day you open an envelope and it changes your life."

He looked perplexed. I explained to him about my soon-to-be-ex-husband's penchant for phone sex and how I'd found out about it by rifling through the bills.

"I'm surprised you would have agreed to turn a blind eye to all the bills," Costa said.

"I was only twenty-one years old. I wanted to be a good wife. I didn't know any better. He wouldn't allow me to even look at the bills, much less handle them. It all became clear why he'd been so adamant about keeping them from me the day I opened the phone bill and discovered his perverse obsession."

"That's sick."

"Well, guess what. It's exactly what I've been doing for the last year with Thof. I really have a knack for repeating past mistakes, don't I?"

"What are you saying? Thof is having phone sex?"

"No! I'm saying I'm being kept away from the bills again.

There's something that Thof does not want me to know. What's the big secret this time?"

Costa's mouth opened as though he was about to say something, but he stopped.

"Look at this bank statement. Tell me I'm seeing double."

Costa scanned the statement. "Yep. We don't pull in a fraction of this."

"Exactly. You know something about this?"

"Look on the bright side. You sure don't have to worry about being able to pay the bill for whatever's going to break down next," he said, avoiding my question.

"I could look at it that way. But I'd be fooling myself. Again. Men, they're all the same."

"Well, you're looking at one. I'm not 'one of those men,' Niki."

"Sorry, I didn't mean it that way. It's just been my experience. Now I'm gun-shy, always waiting for the next shoe to drop. If I'm a part of Koraki, like Thof keeps telling me I am, I'm going to insist he put my name on the account. This is ridiculous. When anything happens like the exhaust breaking down, my hands are tied. He used to be on top of paying the monthly bills, too—the vendors, you, me—but with him gone more and more they're getting pushed out sixty or even ninety days sometimes by the time he gets around to paying them. You and I may be able to live with that, but not the vendors. They're starting to grouse."

"Talk to him when he gets home. But be happy it's not the other way around—a zero missing. Now that would be something to worry over."

"You're right, I suppose. Well, we better start setting up. It's good to be back, Costa. Crank some music; let's get this place open."

Costa always had a way of making me feel better, of smoothing things over. I wondered for a second if it was him I was supposed to be with.

12

Thof had been gone for six weeks this time. Each trip seemed to be longer than the last and each time he came and went, the transition got rockier. Just when I had adjusted to him being gone, he came home, and each time I finally got used to him being home, he left. With each coming and going the tension rose.

"Why must we fight every time you go in and out that door?" I asked.

"Because you have to switch gears?"

"That's not fair, Thof. I'm not the one leaving."

"So you want me to stay home? Let my father's business die? For what he's worked so hard for so many years?"

"No, you know I don't mean that. It's just that… I don't know."

"It's just that… I'm interfering in your life here with Costa, isn't it?"

"My gawd. Please don't go there. He and I spend every single day together. What do you expect? We're like brother and sister."

"Right, I know that Greek tragedy. Don't forget, we wrote the book."

"Come on. I don't question you about your business. Surrounded by exotic women bowing at your feet, kowtowing to you. Remember, we met in a bar after all, and that's where you spend most of your time, only five thousand miles away."

"Let's not do this again. I've told you a million times, I meet owners and buyers. It's a day job. I'm not hanging out at bars all night."

I thought I had better let it go. After all, I was having my cake and eating it, too. I had no right to question him. Whatever came my way I deserved.

"There's something else I've been meaning to ask you about," I said.

Thof rolled his eyes and sighed. "Go on."

"Is it all so bad? Don't roll your eyes at me!"

"Sorry. Go on."

"Well, there are money issues. The first is that I couldn't help noticing the amount of money in the bar's bank account."

"What are you doing in the account?"

"When I got back from Turkey, there was a giant stack of mail to go through. I literally ripped through it all and accidentally opened the bank statement that had also accidentally been delivered there. You seem more concerned that I opened it than what I'm trying to tell you."

"Well, I can't say without seeing it. I'll take a look tomorrow. I'm sure it's either a bank error or you're misreading it."

"You take me for an idiot? I do have a college degree, Thof, and I've seen a few bank statements in my life. Greek numbers look the same as American numbers."

"I didn't mean it that way and you know it. Listen, I brought home a special bottle and a little something for you. Why don't we open it now? There's plenty of time to deal with this later."

He always knew how to soften me, not to mention change the subject.

"Okay. Just let me give Costa a call and make sure he's doing okay by himself."

"Costa is fine. If there's a problem, he'll call. He's worked many nights by himself. He's perfectly capable. Let's go up to the roof. It's a gorgeous night."

Times like this I wished I didn't take things so seriously. So what if I didn't have control over the money, so what if I was having a fling with Costa, so what if I didn't know everything about Thof—the decisions he'd made, what he chose to tell me or not tell me. I'd made a bold leap in my life coming here to be with him. I didn't have a care in the world, and I was living in a slice of paradise. These thoughts tended to swing on the pendulum further in opposite directions every time something came up. The more I tried to let it go one day, the more I'd latch on to it with a pit bull's grip the next day. Where was the middle ground? I needed to find my balance in the center of the boat.

Thof had prepared everything. The wine and glasses were already on the table, along with fresh melon and prosciutto slices, figs with sheep cheese drizzled with sticky thick hundred-year-old balsamic vinegar, and my favorite bread from the local baker.

"Oh! Beautiful!"

"You deserve it. Come on; sit."

He opened the bottle expertly. I watched him elegantly cut the foil and cork the bottle with such grace and subtle flair. Why was it such a masculine act, I wondered. Sensuous in some odd way. Like a service he was performing for me.

"Niki, you know I miss you so much when I'm gone. I think of you all the time. I can never wait to get back."

"I miss you, too. It's so hard. I feel like we drift so far from each other every time."

"But don't you feel me when I'm gone? I'm sending you energy all the time."

"That's kind of a long way for energy to travel."

"It's not, though. It's instantaneous. It's not like it has to take a plane. It's the same as if we were ten feet apart. That's how powerful it is. Have you forgotten?"

"I guess I have, a bit. I haven't really been practicing it.

Days go by and I don't even have time to catch a breath, much less practice."

"You should keep it up. Don't lose our light."

We drank and ate. He told me stories about his travels. "Pour yourself the last glass now," he said.

I picked up the bottle, offering him some first.

"No, no; I'm fine. You have it. It's special," he said.

I tilted the bottle and poured the last of the wine. "What's that?" I asked.

"What?"

"Did you hear that clinking? There's something in the bottle."

"What? Of course there's not. How could there be?" Thof teased.

I emptied the last bit of wine into my glass, and something came tumbling out of the bottle and splashed into the glass.

"What the hell? Do you see that?"

"What is it?"

I tilted my glass and saw two objects glimmering through the wine. "Thof! Did you do this?"

"I wanted to surprise you."

"How did you do that?"

"Oh, a little trick I have."

I fished the earrings out of the wine and rinsed them in my glass of sparkling water.

"I hope you like them. The settings are palladium, and the diamonds virtually have superpowers of their own."

"I love them!" He had a knack for picking out the best jewelry, unlike most men, who wouldn't have a clue. "You're the one with superpowers. Thank you."

"You deserve it."

"That's the second time tonight you said that to me."

"Is it?"

We made our animal love in the cool air, and he reminded me how he'd ensnared me the first time we'd made love. It seemed like yesterday.

13

We got to Koraki early the next morning before Costa arrived. I showed off the new exhaust system to Thof.

"Wow, you meant what you said. I'm impressed. You did this all yourself?"

He turned the switch on and off, on and off. Why did that annoy me so much?

"I got the ball rolling, you could say. Otherwise, I'd have to give the credit to your dad."

"I'll be sure to thank him when I see him today," Thof said. "I know how hard it must have been for you to approach him on that. But I bet he was secretly happy to do it for you."

"Secretly smug is more like it. Anyway, it finally got finished, thanks to him. Now I know what angle to approach these things from the next time something happens. And speaking of that… please don't roll your eyes now; I'm still glowing from last night," I smiled. "Here's that accidental bank statement." I winked, playing with him, hoping to keep the conversation light.

"Sure. I'll take it with me. Get it straightened out." He folded it up and shoved it in his back pocket.

"Uh, wait. I thought we could go over it together."

"Damn it, Niki. Would you let it go?"

"Let what go? All I'm asking is to look at a piece of paper together. What's going on with you? You're acting like you're hiding something."

"There you go again. I'm not your ex-husband."

"Ex. That's right. There's another thing I forgot to tell you."

"Oh, hell." And this time he did roll his eyes.

"I got divorce papers from Jin. And ironically, they were delivered by your father. Talk about weird."

"I don't see how that's weird."

"Never mind. It's not the point."

"What is your point?"

"Nothing. I just thought you should know."

"Are you upset about it?" Thof asked.

"Honestly, I'd put it… him… out of my mind, so yes, it was a bit of a shock, a wake-up call, I suppose."

"A wake-up call to what?"

"To everything I've done. Since the day we met—Pema, you coming to Portland, me running away. Guilt."

"Aren't you happy?"

"Of course I'm happy, but that doesn't preclude me from thinking about what kind of person it makes me appear to be."

"You don't appear to be anything other than the wonderful person you are. So get over it, sweetheart. Did you sign the papers?"

"No, I threw the envelope on top of all the other mail that had piled up while I was gone."

"Hey, guys. Hey, Thof. Good to see you again." Costa straggled into the bar, wrinkled shirt, tousled hair, unshaven. "Welcome home. Am I interrupting something?"

It was always awkward for me when the three of us were together. On the one hand, Costa and I were such great friends, but on the other, we had to be so careful with our glances and our naturally flirtatious talk. It was such a betrayal to Thof. The best thing to do was act naturally. I'd made it clear to Costa that I wasn't going to leave Thof. Costa was the marrying kind. In fact, what he wanted most was a barnful of kids. I'd never really wanted kids, so even if I left Thof, he and I were at an impasse. Knowing the reality of it didn't make it any easier, though. I'd made my bed, now I had to sleep in it. And it was getting pretty crowded.

"Costa, you old dog. You look like hell. What's her name?" Thof asked.

Costa caught my eye and saw me stiffen. He'd cut the cord.

"Remember Brielle?" Costa asked Thof.

"*The* Brielle?" Thof asked.

"Who's Brielle?" I asked.

"Wow. Elly goes way back. I mean to the way, way back. We met in polytech. She was premed, put herself through school stripping. Smart and beautiful. You're one lucky bastard, Costa." Thof slapped him on the back.

"You left out some of the story, though," Costa said. "He forgot to say, they were quite the item back then." Costa's gaze burned a hole through me.

"What's wrong, Niki?" Thof put his hand on my shoulder and laughed. "It was another lifetime, babe."

"Another planet," Costa added. "I don't remember the half of it. We were so boxed out of our heads. My advice, if you ever want good shit, get it from a reliable source—a premed student."

"So what's ol' Elly up to these days? How the hell did you run into her?"

"She actually came into the bar last night. Said she was looking for you. One thing led to another."

"Me?" Thof shifted his weight and took his hand off my shoulder.

"Yeah. She said she had something for you."

"Me?"

"Your needle is skipping, Thof," I said, not sure who or what to be most upset about. I'd have to make a list.

"No, I just can't believe it. It's so weird. I haven't thought about her in years. Why would she have something for me?"

"Hell if I know, pal. I skipped over that part. Ended up she had something for me, too. Wink wink." Costa made a clicking sound with his tongue. "Giddyup."

"Gawd," I said, feeling smaller and smaller by the minute.

"What's wrong?" Thof asked.

"Nothing. Absolutely nothing." I tried to keep my voice steady.

"You're jealous, aren't you?" Thof asked me.

"Of what?"

"Of Elly. I mean Brielle," Thof said.

"Oh, stop. I'm disgusted by how you two talk about it."

"If you say so."

"Listen, I have a lot on my mind right now in case you haven't noticed," I said.

"Yes, all your envelopes," Thof said smugly.

"You're not helping, Thof. What does this Brielle, I mean Elly, have for you?" I asked.

"Hell if I know. I haven't even seen her in ten years."

"Well, that's pretty odd, wouldn't you say?"

"Yes, I would say," Thof retorted.

"I should really get started opening," I said.

"Go ahead. I have to check in with Dad. See you tonight?" Thof asked. "Sure." I waited for Thof to leave and turned on some dark, moody music.

"You're pretty pissed, I'm sure," Costa said. He could see my tears welling up.

"Pissed? More like furious, hurt, and humiliated! I feel like I just got it from both ends. Thof is so patronizing with his old-fashioned attitude about money, then he's practically patting me on the head like a child over Brielle, totally marginalizing any feelings I might have about it. Then you… finding out this way that you rocked her boat," I said as snarkily as I could. "I don't know if I should cry or scream or run away."

"I'm sorry," he took me in his arms. "After Cesme… well, I thought maybe you were right. Brielle happened in by pure chance last night. It was awkward for me talking about it like that just now. Maybe I was getting back at you."

"Why do I keep ending up in this situation? If I bring up a concern, I'm complaining. If I ask for help, I'm needy. I'm never enough to hold someone's attention, so I find someone new. I thought it was different with Thof. He can be so attentive, so empathic, then the next thing I know he's gone, doing who knows what. You're my best friend Costy, *and* my new distraction."

"I'll always be here for you. You know that."

"Damn you." I punched his chest weakly and forced a laugh. He hugged me tighter. "Come on. We'd better get back to it. We have a bunch of deliveries waiting out back."

I wiped my face and forced myself to compartmentalize. Work was the best distraction. I knew I'd get over him sleeping with her eventually. I'd be sad, but wasn't going to collapse into a quivering puddle of tears. Everything else—the envelopes and Brielle's unknown delivery—made it seem worse than it had to be.

"Costa, seriously, what do you know about this Brielle? What does she want with Thof?" I asked as angst-ridden Alanis Morisette thrummed darkly through the speakers.

"Only what I said about knowing her in college."

"She was your drug dealer, though?"

"Oh, yeah. Everyone knew she was a good source. All kinds of stuff. Pills, mostly."

"Well, what's she doing now?"

"She said she's a pharmaceutical rep."

"Oh, nice. How perfect. I can only imagine what kind of side business she's got going."

"Well, if she does, that'd be pretty stupid. I mean, the odds of getting caught seem pretty high and I imagine the penalties would be huge. Anyway, I hear they make a load of money, so I doubt she'd need to supplement it."

"It always seems the more people make, the more they want. Ever notice that? It's like they become insatiable. They'll go to all lengths to make more money. I obviously do not have that problem." I was finally starting to relax. "How long ago did you say that Thof was with her?"

"Niki, you're not thinking what I think you're thinking, are you?"

"I'm curious is all."

"It was ten years ago. I remember because they admitted him on his birthday."

"Wait, what do you mean 'admitted him?'"

"Oh, shit. I thought I told you before."

"Told me what, Costa? What happened?"

"Listen, you have to swear to never let on to Thof that I told you. Promise me, Niki."

"You know I won't say anything. I promise."

"I'm only telling you because you have the right to know what you're getting into. We were partying, of course. It was his twenty-second birthday. It was pretty much like any other night since that's all we did—party—except Thof had been pretty moody lately. A bunch of us were down by the river, under the bridge, throwing bottles and shit—being dumb asses—when Thof started yelping. It was funny at first. We all joined in, but then he wouldn't stop. We couldn't stand it anymore and tried to get him to stop. It kind of started a fight. That's when he ran off. We found out the next day the police had picked him up. He'd been running through the streets naked and apparently talking in some language no one could decipher. More like yapping. They sent him to a psych ward. Which I suppose was a favor. Better than jail."

"Oh my gawd. How long was he in for?"

"Well, that was the beginning of the end, you could say. I mean, he was in and out for the next two years. At first, they'd pick him up and forcefully admit him, but eventually he admitted himself. I think his dad forced him in once, too. In the end, he must have found help in there because he seemed to have emerged clean. One day he walked out and never went back—to that dark place in his head or to the ward."

"So you can understand then why someone like Brielle showing up would concern me?" I asked.

"When you put it that way, yeah. But Niki, you shouldn't go down that path."

"I get the impression the path is quite narrow, and it wouldn't take much to step off."

"We all want to forget about that time. It wasn't fun. No one knew if he'd make it."

"It makes me really nervous."

"I understand, but it's been ten years now. I think he's changed since then."

"You're probably right. But what's up with Brielle? I doubt it was a pizza she was delivering."

"I guess we'll just have to wait and see. I'm glad to see you have your sense of humor back, Nik Nik." It was like an invisible hug when he called me my pet name.

"I'd say she's my number three."

"What do you mean?"

"You know, when things happen in threes? Three knocks, three-headed beasts. You should know about that."

"You're so full of woo, Nik Nik. So what are your three?"

"Number one: the bank statement envelope I opened; number two: the envelope Ugo delivered with my divorce papers; and number three: Brielle. What do you bet she's delivering an envelope?"

"You're quite the detective. But wait. Is that what I interrupted this morning when I came in? You two talking about the divorce papers?"

"Yeah, that and the bank statement, which Thof is being very cagey about. He shoved it in his back pocket and said he'd take care of it. On top of it, the divorce papers seem to have sucker punched me. I'm going to have to deal with them."

"Well, I'm glad I'm not on your list. That would make four."

"I've moved you to a different list. You're off the three-headed beast list and back on the best friend list. I can't afford it any other way."

"Nik Nik."

"Costy." I threw a wet dish towel at him and we attacked

each other in a laughing tangle of tickling, like kittens playing.

"Stop! Stop! I'm going to pee my pants, Costy!"

"I should nick your panties then, Nik Nik."

"Excuse me?" 'Jesus' knocked at the open door. "Sorry to intrude. Just delivering your clean towels."

We jumped up, straightening our clothes. "*Efaristo, efaristo*," we both said at the same time, stifling laughter. *Thank you, thank you.*

"He's always sneaking around! Shit. That will be on the front page of the paper tomorrow," I said.

Finally we got back to work, prepping to open. I changed the music to Kris Kross, "Jump." What a bunch of brats, I thought, but the music got me hip-hopping around the floor, waking up my energy for the night ahead. Spring had sprung.

14

It was an average spring night at Koraki. Midweek. A nice break from all the craziness that the weekend trippers bring. It gave the locals a chance to stop in and hang out.

Costa was straightening up behind the bar when I saw him pull an envelope out from between two stacks of plates.

"Oh, shit," he said under his breath. He folded it in half and shoved it in his back pocket.

"What's that?" I asked.

"Nothing."

"Yes, it is. I can see it," I teased.

"Just something I forgot about."

"Let me see. I saw you pull it from the shelf." I put my arms around him and tried to reach for his back pocket.

"Niki, I said it's nothing!" he said sharply.

The customers sitting at the bar oohed and aahed jokingly. They were used to seeing us playacting and dancing around behind the bar. I grabbed a towel, spun it into a tight roll and snapped it at him. It cracked loudly, stinging him on the leg.

"Hey! Knock it off. That really hurts!" Costa grabbed his own towel and I got him on the arm. "Ow!" He turned and ran out from behind the bar, and I snatched the envelope from his pocket, crumpled it into my own pocket and went after him with more towel snaps. The customers howled with laughter as Costa feigned frailty, which spurred Magnificent Sperm Man, always vying for attention, to pull out his ukulele and strum an improvised love song. He swooned over the women sitting at the bar who giggled to cover their embarrassment for him.

When the last customers of the night left and Costa had gone early, too, I was left to myself. If he'd planned on getting the envelope back, he must have forgotten after all the commotion. I poured myself a large glass of wine, sat down on the leather sofa, and put my feet up on the low table. I'd changed the seating when I took over for Thof, replaced the ubiquitous wobbly wooden chairs with comfy love seats and throw pillows, positioning them in a half circle to face the music when bands played. Customers loved the living room feeling. They finally had a place to huddle in small groups to gossip and drink French wine. Every place else in town served generic, mass-produced wine from gallon jugs.

I pulled the crumpled envelope out of my pocket. It was addressed to Thof in a girlish, scrolly handwriting: "Thof XXOO." So here it was, the third envelope, just like I'd predicted. I couldn't believe it. I could feel my heart pounding in my chest, a staccato pulse rising into my throat. I'd been here before with Jin: the truth staring me in the face. All I had to do was press a computer key, open an envelope, or study a phone bill to learn something I really didn't want to know. Should I do it now? Again? Live with the guilt for snooping, then test him with my new-found information? Dropping hints and asking vague questions, hoping that whatever he told me would lessen the gravity of what I'd found? Prove me wrong? But it never worked out that way. It only made things worse.

I carefully opened the envelope, trying not to tear it. Inside was a small piece of paper with the same handwriting—*Try it, you'll like it. Let me know*—and three pills: an oval gelcap, a dark purple pill so small I almost missed it, and a round yellow pill with a happy face on it. I'd seen the yellow one before, with its signature stamp—Ecstasy. It was common to see it passed around at parties and bars. If I didn't know any better, I'd swear the oval gelcap was a vitamin D pill, but the itty-bitty one, I had no clue. I wasn't prepared for this. I'd been expecting a love letter, a proposition of some sort. I had no experience with drugs. It was one subject that I was naive about. It made me sick to my stomach thinking about it. Why was Brielle passing pills to Thof? I made a mental note of the shape and color of the pills. I'd research them later. Now, though, I resealed the envelope as best I could. It was completely wrinkled from being in Costa's and my pockets.

I finished my wine and walked up the hill to stand above the water before heading home. I needed time to process this before seeing Thof at home. How should I present the envelope to him? Just leave it on the counter for him to find in the morning? Hand it to him with a wry smirk? I had to have faith there was nothing going on. It was an old joke, I tried to convince myself. In my mind I ran through the story Costa had told me about Thof's breakdown. What kind of drugs was he using then? I hadn't asked. I decided to keep it simple—tell Thof that Costa had found the envelope on the shelf. Give him the benefit of the doubt. I suddenly felt overwhelmed with exhaustion.

Passing the bar again on my way home, I saw a light on in the back. I was certain I'd turned them all off. I found the key in my pocket and slid it into the lock, but the door was unlocked already.

"Hello?" I yelled, not sure why, and headed toward the light in the backroom. A scuffling sound came from behind the bar. I stopped in my tracks, automatically took a step backwards, and knocked two bottles together on the wine shelves. I froze. The noise behind the bar stopped. It was all happening in slow motion, yet in a split second. Slowly a head rose from behind the bar. Hair, forehead, eyebrows. I was pinned up against the wine wall.

"Costa! You scared me to death! What are you doing?" I hollered.

"What are _you_ doing? You scared the hell out of me!" he shouted back.

"I took a walk after I closed and saw the light on when I came back."

"Where's the envelope, Niki?"

"Right here. I have it. Is that what you're doing here? Looking for it? What is so goddamned important about this envelope, Costa?"

"Thof was… I mean, it just slipped my mind today and I remembered I never gave it to him," he said.

"Must be awfully important for you to get out of bed at two a.m. to come back here for it."

"No, I couldn't sleep, so I thought I'd come pick it up before I forgot again."

"Well, I already opened it."

"Niki!"

"It has pills in it and a note that says, 'Try it, you'll like it.'"

"What?" Costa asked incredulously.

"Tell me you didn't know what was in it," I said. This bullshit was really starting to piss me off. I could feel the heat rising in my cheeks.

"Niki, I had no clue. I swear to God. Let me see."

"No, I already resealed it. It's barely holding shut as it is. You gotta help me out on this one."

"I had no idea, I told you. Maybe it's a joke. Some inside joke from school days."

"Brielle must have told you something the night you two—" I trailed off.

"Oh shit, I'm embarrassed about how fucked up I was that night. I couldn't remember if I wanted to."

"I bet you were."

"Come on, Nik."

"Yeah, yeah, whatever. It's the pills I'm concerned with now. You don't think…" I hesitated.

"Listen, there's stuff I haven't told you."

"Damn it! You just said that a few days ago! Now what?"

"It's late, Nik. Are you sure this is what you want now?"

"Hell yes! Sit down and start talking!"

…

Brielle was three years ahead of Costa and Thof in college. She'd started out as premed but couldn't stomach the cadavers and dropped "down" to chemistry. She was no dummy, though. When she graduated, magna cum laude, she got a job as a pharmacist. The low salary wasn't worth the whining patients and strangling insurance companies, so she became a rep. It was much more up her alley—partying with coworkers who didn't hesitate to experiment with the goods, and with doctors with huge expense accounts who no longer felt the need to play God with her and who were very happy with her anatomy. She never imagined the shameless saleswoman she could be.

Thof and Costa hadn't even graduated yet and she was making millions selling subgrade, imported tramadol, opioid pain meds, to physicians. She was greedy for even more money, though, and living more and more on the wild side, meeting shady people. She wanted to be a producer—but this time the real thing, LSD. She recruited Thof to blaze the trail for her. His first scouting trip had been to Singapore. They'd done the research and decided it was the safest place to start, not to mention the richest. If he got caught, he wouldn't end up tortured and rotting in a rat-infested prison cell like he might in Thailand or Sri Lanka.

"So thoughtful of her," I interjected. "I can't believe he'd stoop that low. She must've had some influence on him. I've never met her, and I already hate her."

The Singaporean government had a heavy hand, but for the most part they were still civil. But that heavy hand raised a generation of hyper-succeeders who were young, rich, and super smart but starving for an outlet. At the time, chewing gum and kissing in public would land you in jail, so it was no surprise to find underground clubs where the young let loose. There also happened to be a booming wine market there. Young Asians were looking to the West for the latest fads in everything from music to alcohol to drugs. Every generation wants to set their own trends and this one was making it with wine. By then, Thof's dad had started producing his own wine again. The vineyard that had been in Thof's mom's family for generations had been fallow for years after she died. Ugo wanted to make a go of it.

Thof was in the right place at the right time and took advantage of it—advantage of the hip twenty-somethings, too. He was tripping and flipping out right alongside them while delivering their drugs of choice. Sometimes he'd even throw in an exceptional bottle of wine. They went nuts over that. They loved Thof's style. Opposite of the loud, brash, and stumbling Westerner they were accustomed to, he had the Zen vibe going. He got into private clubs, passing through the gatekeeper's turf like a snake in the grass. Slippery and quiet. He entered through the back door with his goods—a case of wine loaded with just a quarter ounce of LSD, enough for 100,000 doses—and left through the front door, hands empty, pockets lined. LSD was the most expensive drug, conversely related to its size and weight. A microdot, about the size of the head of a pin, would provide a twelve-hour high.

"But where did Brielle get it?" I asked.

"God knows, but Thof was having the time of his life. He was also having more episodes like the one I told you about before when he got admitted. Brielle was satisfied with his progress, though. He was her guinea pig now. And Thof's dad didn't care enough to question the unwarranted success of his wine; he was out of his mind happily counting the cash. No one was looking out for Thof."

"Why did you wait so long to tell me?"

"I wanted to many times. It's such a betrayal to Thof. He would kill me if he found out I told you. But you're more important now."

"Jesus! I'm speechless. Are you serious? I mean, he'd literally kill you? And what do you mean, a case of wine loaded with LSD?"

"There were some things he didn't tell me. I think to absolve me. So I don't know. I do know that I love you, Niki. I don't want to see you hurt. In spite of it all, Thof's my friend and it would be really hard for me to believe that he's back in the game, but I just can't risk it. I can't risk him using you or somehow dragging you into something…"

"Something? My gawd! You think Brielle has sucked him back in? I mean, he's so busy. How would he even have time to do something like that again?"

"No, no, no. See, this is what I didn't want to happen. I didn't want to scare you. Just give him the envelope and let him tell you. I'm sure it's not going to be anything. Maybe I shouldn't have said anything. It was a long time ago," Costa said.

"This is going to take some time to sink in. How do you know all this?"

"Thof and I were like brothers. I was the only one he could talk to. Through it all—the drugs and his episodes, he trusted me."

"You always think the best of everyone. I wish I was that way."

"I assume people have the best intentions. It doesn't always end up that way, but I think they mostly start out that way."

"How'd you end up with such a cheery outlook?"

"I'd have to give my mom the credit for that. In fact, I'm going to visit her tomorrow. Why don't you come along? I think the two of you would hit it off. She could help you sort all this out. What's that Disney movie of yours? Sugar helps the medicine go down?"

"Or in this case, three little pills. Yes, just a spoonful," I said.

"I'll pick you up at noon. Now go home and get some sleep."

"Right. There's some wishful thinking.

...

I left the envelope on the kitchen counter for Thof to pick up in the morning and slid into bed beside him. I told myself it was all a joke.

I dreamed I was on a large cruise ship. It rocked violently back and forth in a storm. The waves were huge. A doctor was giving a talk about his research on why my spine hurt so much. He was projecting slides of my X-rays. They were colorful and three-dimensional. He pointed out all the sharp little bony spindles that had grown along the edges of my vertebrae. They looked like fish bones, fine and wispy. He plucked one right off the projected image and said, "These will all have to be removed. One by one. Osteochondromatosis. Usually only seen in canines." Suddenly the ship turned over and all was panic and mayhem. Passengers were climbing over a metal railing, disappearing into a dark, murky pool of water. Pema was in the middle of it, beckoning me in. I climbed over the railing and immersed myself in the water, not knowing how I'd see underwater to follow her or how far I'd have to swim. Finally we surfaced in a bright shiny pool where Pema's baby girl was cooing and playing in the water like a dolphin.

I woke late and felt as though I hadn't slept at all. My eyes were puffy and the lines in my face seemed exaggerated. I padded out to the kitchen, made coffee, and fed the cat. The balcony doors were open, and the sun filtered through the sheer curtains billowing in the breeze. Another day in paradise, I reminded myself. A note on the counter beside my coffee cup read:

> N.
>
> Let's meet for lunch today. XXOO
>
> T.

The envelope was gone.

Shit. I'd promised Costa I'd go with him to visit his mother.

The cat rubbed against my legs.

"Minky, baby, tell me what to do." I picked her up, nuzzled my face into her neck, and called Costa. "Can we leave after lunch? Thof wants to have lunch with me. I have to."

"Sure. Just ring me when you're done. Don't be forever, please."

"Thanks. You're a dear," I told Costa.

"I knew you'd know what to do," I told the cat and let her jump down. She stretched out in the sun on the balcony, the tip of her tail waving a lazy hello at me. But I felt nervous and jittery. Why couldn't I take a lesson from Minky? Let the world come to me instead of me chasing it around, trying to control everything in my path? That's the wrong direction Niki, I thought. Look at the cat. Take a hint. Minky rolled on her back, swatted at a fly, then closed her eyes and napped.

I dressed to be ready to leave with Costa. I chose a short flippy dress with heavy black boots. They always made me feel tough and grounded, but sexy, too. I scrunched my socks down so you couldn't see them, put on large hoop earrings and more makeup than usual. I wasn't sure if I'd done that for Thof's or Costa's sake. Either way, I needed to feel good about myself. I grabbed a sweatshirt for later when the sun went down. It would be cold on the drive to Costa's mother's. He would insist on having the top down.

"Bye, kitty. See you tonight." I gave Minky a scratch, envying her insouciance.

...

I met Thof at our favorite taverna in the old part of town. We sat outside where the tables were set in the cool, narrow cobblestone alley and cats weaved between your ankles begging for food. There was not a skinny one to be seen.

"Sleep well? You got in late," Thof said.

"No, actually I didn't sleep well at all. I walked to the beach after work. I needed some air."

"You left early this morning."

"Busy busy."

I noticed Thof's eyes had lost their crystal blue color. They were grayer this morning, more like a slatey blue. It was another thing he'd taught me—eyes change color.

"This is nice," I said. "Like the old days." I wasn't looking forward to the conversation we were about to have. I wanted to deny it all, pretend everything was normal.

"It's been too long since we had a relaxing lunch." Thof rearranged his fork and knife. "Listen, I need to tell you that I have to make an unexpected trip to Istanbul at the end of the week. The contact I met the last time I was there… when we all ran into each other"—he narrowed one eye at me—"is actually amounting to something, so I'm popping over there for a few days. Tony, another Anchor," he gestured the waiter with a raised hand and ordered a beer.

"This contact. Her name doesn't happen to be Brielle, does it?"

"Oh, Niki, you have nothing to worry about. You know I love you. You must think more of me than that, don't you?"

"Then why didn't you tell me?"

"Because I knew you'd worry and give me a hard time."

"And now that you didn't tell me, I will worry, so either way, I worry. Can you see that?"

"Look at me, Niki. I promise you I would never do anything to hurt you or betray your trust."

"I'm looking at you and to tell you the truth, I don't see it in your eyes." I could feel the trembling start. Whenever I got upset my entire body trembled. It started in my stomach and traveled up to my neck. Sometimes it was so bad I actually had to put my head in my hands to conceal the tremors. It was embarrassing, and when it got that bad, I'd leave the room or make an excuse to use the bathroom.

I slipped my sweatshirt over my shoulders even though it was hot outside. The weight of it felt good on my back and I launched in.

"What's your story about the envelope, Thof?"

"She was passing through town and when she didn't find me at the bar, like I always used to be, she left a note for me. It's how she used to let us know when her delivery came in. That was ages ago. Anyway, she doesn't know about you. That's how long it's been since I've even seen or talked to her. She's not the kind of person to break up a relationship."

"But you saw her the last time you were in Turkey. What do you mean you haven't seen her since we've been together?"

"It didn't come up, Niki. I was in a hurry. I had a flight to catch; it was strictly business."

"You don't see an old girlfriend for ten years and you're in such a hurry that you don't even tell each other your status? That's a good one, Thof. Would you like to try again? I'll give you another chance to come up with a plausible answer. A story you can stick with." I was determined to let him tell me about the pills on his own. "What else did her note say?"

"Nothing, Niki. That's all it said."

"There are a lot of loose ends in your story." I knew if I took a drink of water my head would tremble as I tilted it back to swallow. I brushed my hair back and massaged my neck. Calm down. Breathe.

"Niki, I love you so much. Please don't do this."

"Me? I'm the one doing this? You need to rethink that one. Are you going to tell me what else was in the envelope, Thof?"

"Did you open it?" He sounded incredulous.

"It opened itself."

"*Ha*! Now it's your turn to explain that one!"

"I was trying to get it from Costa after I saw him pull it from the shelf. I wanted to know what it was since he was so secretive about it. I picked it from his pocket when he turned around and with all the folding and shoving into pockets to hide it, it just came open. It was barely sealed to begin with. So I know about the pills. I wanted to give you a chance to tell me yourself. You flunked."

"So this is all about tests."

"Call it what you like, Thof. You know damn well you had

no intention of telling me any of this. Oh, and I should add to the list, the tremendous amount of money in the bank account. I want my name added to the account. It's way overdue. If… I mean when anything goes wrong, breaks down, or a special event requires extra help, my hands are tied without access to the bank account."

"This is not the time or the place to talk about this, Niki. I wanted to have a nice lunch."

"There is never a good time to talk about this and it will never be convenient. You're always running off to the office, a phone call, or another country."

"I have to go to the bathroom." He threw his napkin on the table. His chair tipped on one leg then skipped around on all four before settling down. Heads turned.

My heart was pounding, and I couldn't hold back the tears. Without a second thought, I ran away from the table and slipped into the corner store where I knew there was a pay phone.

"Costa, I'm done with lunch. Can you come get me now? Quick?"

"Niki, what's wrong?"

"I'll tell you when you get here. Hurry. I'm at Ottika."

"I'll be there in five. The car's all packed. I'm ready to go."

Head down, I rifled through a rack of souvenir T-shirts, pretending to be interested in buying something, avoiding the owner's gaze. I didn't want him to see me crying. It never ceased to amaze me how fast gossip spread around town. I heard every bit of it at the bar and didn't believe for one second that people didn't love to gossip about me, too. I was proud of myself for never participating in it. Sure I contributed *oohs* and *aahs* and shocked *No's*! I wanted to indulge my customers and at the same time make them feel that nothing said there would leave the room. I got the best of both that way—I heard all the gossip and got a modicum of respect. I wondered if I could keep it up, though. As locals started accepting me into the fold, they also started to talk about me. I thought I was above it all. I had a business to run, after all. But soon enough, it got under my skin and kept me awake at night. The next thing I knew, I'd fabricated the most ridiculous lie I could think of—I'd be sponsoring thirteen followers of Macumba, Brazilian black magic worshipers. They'd be camping out in our apartment so the neighbors should guard their chickens and goats. I whispered it to the biggest gossips and off it flew. It was exhilarating. Not to mention hilarious.

…

Finally I saw Costa's yellow Jeep speed around the corner. With my back to the store owner, I waved goodbye and ran out of the store.

"Where's your stuff?" Costa asked.

"Oh, shit. I left it at home. I planned on you picking me up there after lunch. Can we swing by and I'll run in and grab it?"

"Sure, Nik. What's going on? You don't look too good."

"I bet."

I ran up the stairs of our apartment to grab my bag. I opened the door and nearly slipped on the pile of mail that had been pushed through the door slot. I gathered it up and threw it on the counter when a hand-addressed envelope caught my eye. It was from Pema. I contemplated it for a moment before shoving it into my bag and racing back down the stairs to Costa's idling Jeep.

Thof would be furious when he returned from the bathroom at the cafe and found me gone, but I knew him well enough to know he would dive right into work, not ruminate over me one bit. He wouldn't even know I'd left town until he got home later that night.

15

It was just over a two-hour drive to Peristeria, a remote town on the island of Salamis, west of Athens, where Costa's mother lived. Driving into the hills, I didn't stop talking once to take a breath as I recounted Thof's and my lunch to Costa.

"I know I probably shouldn't have left, but he pushed me to my limit. Limit of lies, omissions, and dismissiveness."

"I have to say, it even surprises me," Costa said. "What are you going to do?"

"I have no idea. If he has nothing to hide, like he claims, then why all the secrets? It's driving me mad. I don't have time for this. Life's too short. Did I leave one liar just to end up with another?"

"I can talk to him if you want."

"I don't know. I do know that getting out of town was a great idea, though. Oh my gawd, I almost forgot… I got a letter from Pema! I'm scared to open it."

"Well, we have all the time in the world now. And I bet it's good news. Read it to me."

I held the envelope up toward the sky to see the shadow of what was inside.

"What are you expecting in there?" Costa asked.

"I don't know. Looks like a regular letter to me." I slipped my finger under the sealed flap, and visualized Pema licking the glue parts. I carefully slid my finger along it so as not to tear it, as though it was a precious keepsake.

Niki,

I felt I should let you know that Jin and Bing know everything that's happened—to you, to me. I couldn't live with it anymore, especially since I decided to keep the baby! It was going to become obvious soon enough, so I told Bing and of course he told Jin. Can't really blame him.

Though I must say they are blaming you. Jin was going to be civil and fair with the divorce, but after he heard the story, he is pulling out all the stops to make sure you get no more than the minimum legally due to you. You probably already got the papers. I wanted to let you know that I tried to talk him out of it. I told him what happened to me was in no way your fault (and I really do mean that), but his mind is made up. He's adamant.

Niki, I really hope some day you and I can get past this and be friends again. I've come to terms with it all. If it hadn't been for all that happened between you and Thof, I would not have this beautiful being with me now. I hope I see you again some day and you will meet the baby. (It's a girl!)

Best, Pema

"Oh my gawd, I had a dream that Pema had a baby girl!" I said. "I'm surprised she decided to keep it, though. I suppose she still feels the void of losing her first one, as unplanned as that was also. I don't understand how a woman could go through with it. I mean, wouldn't it be a reminder of being raped for the rest of your life? And to think the likelihood is stunningly high that when she grows up she'll be sexually assaulted too, like her mother. How sweet is that?"

"Wow, you need a vacation, Nik. Either that or a knock with a baseball bat to get those thoughts out of your head," Costa said. "She's reaching out to you."

"Sorry. I shouldn't say those things out loud. Seriously, it's great to hear from her. A relief, actually. I'll write her."

I couldn't believe it had been nearly three years since Pema and I first arrived in Nafplio. That means her baby must be almost two years old. Just amazing.

"In the meantime, Thof informed me today at lunch that he's leaving again! To Brielle! How many times do you think he's done this?"

"Hold on. Do you remember what we were doing when we ran into him in Turkey? May I remind you it was a pretty spectacular weekend until that unfortunate encounter. Anyway, I'm still not convinced that Brielle is anything more than a business acquaintance. Thof's a changed man. He wouldn't cheat on you, much less get into shady dealings."

"I don't like it."

"Let's get my mom's opinion. She's a bit of a soothsayer."

"Oh boy."

Selena was outside when we pulled up, as though she knew exactly when we had turned off the road and started up the long, pitted lane. The Jeep bounced up and down in spite of straddling the largest holes. I felt rattled and was coated in a layer of grime that clung to my sweaty skin. Selena didn't seem to notice and gave me a big hug, as though I was her own daughter.

"Mom, this is Niki, my good friend. Niki, my mom Selena."

"Oh, he's told me so much about you, Niki."

I gave Costa a sideways glance. "He has? Well you shouldn't believe half of it."

Selena's hearty laugh made her shoulders bounce and ample stomach jiggle. She wore an apron over her dress. I bet she put it on when she dressed in the morning and didn't take it off until she put it in the laundry at night. Her shoes were black lace-ups with a little heel. It reminded me of my own grandmother. But her legs were bare, with no stockings—a hint that she was a pragmatic, liberal-minded woman.

Inside, it smelled like my grandmother's house did when she'd spent the day roasting meat and baking pies and bread for a special holiday meal. The entire back side of the house was made up of windows and glass doors that opened up to a view of hills and terraced slopes of olive trees that stretched until they met the bay. A table under the vine-covered trellis was already set.

"Stunning," I said as I accepted a goblet of red wine.

"Sit, sit," Selena offered.

"Oh no, thank you. I've been sitting for hours. This is so lovely."

"Mom found this place after Dad died. She'd been eyeing it for years and it was quite by luck that she was able to buy it," Costa explained.

"It was meant to be, poppet," Selena said to Costa.

"Poppet?" I asked.

"Mom, please," Costa said. "It's a pet name. It's British. Like 'my little love,' sort of."

We filled ourselves with roasted lamb rubbed with rosemary, along with homemade bread and tomato and cucumber salad from the garden and plenty of wine. Costa told Selena about my concerns over Thof.

"Mom's known Thof since we first met at college. He and I used to come back here on all our breaks."

"So you know all about—" I hesitated, not wanting to reveal too much in case she didn't know all of Thof's history.

"Yes, we saw him through all of it," Selena said. "So you're worried about him?"

"There are just too many things, strange things that I think he's keeping from me. The bank account, Brielle, pills."

"Do you love him?"

"I do. He's an amazing man. He's taught me so much, opened my eyes to things I never would have thought I'd be open to. Some pretty crazy things, in fact."

"He has a dark side. It's part of his soul."

"I love that part of him. But drugs can't be part of that equation."

Selena took my hand in hers and closed her eyes. She had a perpetual smile on her face. Her eyebrows quivered and she gently rocked forward and back in her chair as though in a trance. I looked at Costa, who nodded knowingly. The birds twittered and sang. The air smelled of wild thyme and slate. Cats lounged in the cool, dry dirt.

"Perhaps you are right to worry." Selena slowly opened her eyes and patted my hand.

"What do you mean?" I asked.

"Mom senses things. Nothing specific—silhouettes, you might say," Costa explained. "Her grandmother was a *harus-pex*."

"*Hēpatoskōpia*," Selena said. "How do you say, Costa?"

"There are ancient Roman and Greek practices of reading omens by inspecting the liver of sacrificed animals. Of course people consider it an old wives' tale now, but Mom grew up watching her grandmother practice it. Grandmother always told her she had the gift. She never fails to 'see.' It's why her mother named her Selena. It means moon."

"It's a beautiful name," I told her, wanting to know more about that liver thing. "Why the liver?"

"The liver was considered the source of the blood and hence the basis of life itself," Costa explained.

"I can't help inspecting it when I get my lambs in the spring. I'm there when the *sfazo*—"

"Butcher," Costa translated.

"Yes, yes, butcher. When the *sfazo* opens them up. It's become tradition. Little ritual. Everyone gathers round to watch."

"Fascinating," I said, trying to imagine it. Gross, yet fascinating at the same time.

"It keeps my energy flowing for the rest of the year. It's restorative. I mean for my intuition, too." She fluttered her hands around her head. "In my mind I can revisit the reading of the liver when I want to get a feeling for something."

"And this feeling you have about Thof… doesn't bode well?" I asked.

"It feels heavy. I sense danger. I can't say specifically. There's a feeling of…." she hesitated and closed her eyes again. "Sometimes it's hard to tell the difference between things like fear and excitement. There's a swirling. Do you see what I mean?" Selena asked me.

"Yes. Fear can be exciting," I said.

"Like jumping out of an airplane," Costa added.

"Or losing your mind," I said.

"There are some things you can't save other people from. Things they have to work out themselves," Selena said.

"Are you saying that about Thof?"

"I'm afraid so, poppet," Selena touched my hand again.

"It's okay, Nik. I mean, we all have to work our shit out sometimes. Try not to worry," Costa said. "Let's take a walk. I'll show you around the property. Shake this off."

"But we should clear the table, do the dishes," I said.

"Go, go, you kids," Selena said. "It's my work. My treat."

"You boys sure are coddled, aren't you?" I said to Costa as we left.

"Huh?"

"Geez. You don't have a clue. Such a mamma's boy. She slaves all day to feed you without even a thank you or an offer of help from you."

"She likes it that way."

"Men," I feigned exasperation. "Anyway, I'm already in

love with her. She's like the mother I never had."

"She loves you, too. I can tell. I'm sure she'd be happy to add you to her list of orphans."

"I'm sure there's a long list. Who wouldn't want to be gathered into her nest?"

"That's Mom. There were always so many kids running through the house I grew up in. She loved it that way. She always wanted a full house of her own, but when she found out she couldn't, she kept it filled with other people's kids. So it kind of felt like I grew up with a lot a brothers and sisters."

"That's sad and sweet at the same time."

"Like you are now. Try not to worry, poppet." We folded into each other's arms and kissed.

"Damn you." I punched him on the arm.

"Sorry. Couldn't help myself."

"Please don't."

We made lazy love under the olive trees. The crickets began their chirping, and from a distance the cats kept an eye on us as the sun started its descent behind the hills.

"Are you going to call Thof? Tell him it's too late to drive back tonight?" Costa asked me back at the house.

"I suppose I should. He's probably home by now." I found the phone in Selena's kitchen. "No answer. I left a message. I wonder where he is," I pondered.

"Try again later," Costa suggested.

"No, he can call here if he wants to talk. Let's get back to your mom." The three of us talked and drank late into the night. The phone never rang.

"I'm not looking forward to the reception I'm going to find back home," I said as we made our way back to Nafplio after breakfast. "Costa, why do we keep torturing ourselves with sex?" I asked.

"You don't beat around the bush, do you? Geez."

"Come on, we both know it's wrong. We need to stop. Thof's your friend, not to mention your boss. Ha! That's about as low as a friend can go."

"You're right. I know. You're just so damned sweet."

"Stop, Costa!"

"Okay, okay. I didn't think you meant starting right this second."

"You're hilarious, but help me out here a little. I can't do this myself. Think of it as going on a diet. I'll be your diet buddy. Just so happens we're the forbidden food. Promise?"

"Promise," he agreed.

16

I expected Thof to be at work when I got back to town. I wasn't ready to face another confrontation and was hoping to avoid the inevitable as long as possible. Instead, I found him at home, in the middle of the day, filthy, in jeans and an old T-shirt covered in wine stains. Not his usual pressed linens that Jesus delivered to him weekly. There was glass all over the floor. Minky was behind the sofa.

"What's going on?" I asked, scanning the room looking for clues, feeling a slow panic rising in my chest. "Minky's hiding. Stop pacing, for Christ's sake; you're stepping in the glass." I tiptoed across the room, avoiding the broken wine glass to get the broom.

"Where the hell have you been? I'm the one who should be doing the questioning here, not you!" Thof exploded.

"I called last night but you didn't answer. Didn't you get my message?"

"I've been busy, if you can't tell. No, I didn't get your message!" he yelled.

"What happened? You're a wreck."

"The new wine production has been destroyed." He held his head in his hands. "I went in early this morning because I couldn't sleep and found all the bottles smashed."

"Oh my gawd. Did you call the police?"

"Of course. They told me to leave until they send more officers out later today to investigate. I thought Dad was going to have a heart attack. He's under observation at the clinic. They say it's just a panic attack."

"Shit! Who would do that?" I sat down beside him.

He banged his fist on the table, making the flower vase jump and almost tip over. Minky shot out the balcony doors. Pacing again, he tore his shirt off, ranting to himself and mumbling like a crazy person talking to voices in his head. "Where were you last night?"

"I went with Costa to visit his mother. I told him earlier I'd go along with him. I planned to tell you, but then things got out of hand at lunch. So I just left. I needed to get away."

"And I needed you, Niki. Did you ever think about that? You don't go running off when things get rough around the edges."

"Lunch felt like more than just rough around the edges, Thof. How could I have anticipated something terrible would happen? I'm sorry I ran out on you. I can't believe someone would do this. Did the police tell you anything?"

"They're clueless. Worthless."

"It's all destroyed?"

"All of it that was in the store. Thank God we didn't finish bottling it all. There's still some left in the tanks. The police have to check that, too. Make sure they weren't tampered with. It looks like a real hack job. I can't imagine anyone who did this would have the know-how to get into the tanks, too."

"Your dad must be crushed."

"You can't even imagine. It almost killed him, Niki." Thof swiped my coffee cup off the counter this time and sent it flying across the room. "Damn you, Niki! Another night with Costa. How was it this time?" He kept flip-flopping between rage over the wine and rage at me.

"I told you we went to visit his mother. Don't even go there." I justified it in my head since I knew it was really over this time between Costa and me. I could speak with a clear conscience, as though the affair never happened. How else could I ever live with myself? Men do it all the time. Why should I torture myself because I'm a woman? I argued with myself.

"We talked about you most of the time," I explained. "You never told me you spent so much time there."

"Oh, great, now you're talking about me. What business is it of Selena's that you have to go and talk to her?"

"Thof, she loves you. She considers you like a son. I was worried about you. I needed to talk. Costa told me she knows things."

"What a load of crap. I've heard that so many times. It's bullshit, Niki. I'm sorry you wasted your time."

"I can't believe you'd talk that way about her. She's seriously concerned."

"What could she possibly be concerned about? I haven't seen her in two years. What the hell did you tell her?"

"Calm down. I was asking her for advice, for help. You act as though I was gossiping about you."

"Calm down? You're telling me to calm down? That takes the cake, Niki." He pushed through the French doors to the balcony, slamming them into the wall. They bounced back and slammed shut behind him. Through the closed doors I heard him yelling and cursing at the top of his lungs, shouting into the streets. But the shouting turned into a shrill barking. Like a screaming dog. He leaned over the railing, his back so broad, muscles flaring. The railing flexed with the weight of him pushing against it. People stopped in the street and looked up at him. They stared, mouths agape. Mothers pushed their children along to get them away from the crazy man on the balcony who might fling himself over the railing at any second. They remembered the rumors of ten years ago about a man running through the streets naked, howling like a dog.

I opened the balcony doors.

"Thof, stop! You're scaring me." I tried to pull him inside, off the balcony. I grabbed his arm which was suddenly covered in long hair, but he pushed me back hard enough that I stumbled backwards and fell, lodging a piece of stray glass into the palm of my hand. The sight of blood snapped him out of his raging tantrum. He rushed to me, yanked the glass out of my hand and pressed his mouth against the slash in my palm. But he wasn't putting pressure on it to stop the bleeding, he was sucking the blood out instead. Drinking it. It calmed him like a screaming baby who finds a nipple to nurse on. His eyes were the brightest blue I'd ever seen.

"Niki, please don't leave me. I need you."

"I'm not leaving you," I said, thinking that Selena was right. I needed to decide how much I was willing to live with.

"Come on, let's take a shower. You smell like you fell into a vat. And now you have blood on you." I helped him off the floor with my good hand. "I may have to join your dad at the clinic later, and get this checked out."

His rage had seemed out of control. Over the top. I kept running it over and over in my mind. I could have sworn he was yelping like a dog or screeching like a prehistoric bird. I couldn't begin to recognize the sound. He had almost trilled. And his physical body was inexplicably canine.

I led him in by the scruff of his neck into the shower. The bathroom filled with steam in billowy clouds. His head lolled. Our foreheads touched as the water poured down on us. Blood circled the drain. When he lifted his head, his blue eyes blinked at me as though he was coming out of a dream.

"Niki, you need to wrap your hand. Let me do it for you," he said, turning off the water. This time it was he who led me and sat me down at the kitchen table to tape a towel around it.

Dressed and bandaged, we went to the shop to see the mess. The door jamb was splintered where a crowbar was used to break the bolt. The floor was a sea of broken bottles and red wine, the smell pungent.

"Only the red wine was smashed. No liquor, no white wine. Only the red," Thof explained. "It makes no sense. The cash register is untouched. It's a disaster. I can't believe it. This can't be random."

"I need to let Costa know that I won't be in today. I'll help you with this mess," I said.

"No, I can't touch it until the police are done. Nothing we can do about it. You may as well go to work."

"Only if you're positive. You can always call, and I'll leave Costa on his own. You know that."

"I want you to come to Turkey with me on this trip, Niki. I don't want to be away from you again. We could use some time away. I canceled my trip to Seoul. I'll have to postpone it until we get more bottling done anyway. They'll just have to wait."

"What about your meeting with Brielle?"

"It's one meeting, a dinner, probably. Then we'll have the rest of the weekend to ourselves."

"Uh, well, sure, if that's what you want. I don't want to cramp your style," I said, but my mind was racing in the opposite direction. Nothing had been resolved since our disastrous lunch. Selena had planted a seed of fear in me, and now there was the break-in and Thof's wild behavior. I needed some answers, and fast.

"Niki, please. Be serious. I don't want to be alone."

"Is something else wrong? It feels like there's more." I didn't dare push him but I sensed he was holding back.

"On top of all of this, I'm feeling the full moon agitation coming on," he said.

And there it was—the dark side of the moon. He'd left out the details of that part of his werefox stories until now. It had all been about entwining energies, ecstatic sex, and shifting eye color, not losing his mind. I thought of the pills in Brielle's envelope. Had he taken one (or more), pushing him to the brink? I never would have believed his virtual physical transformation if anyone had told me.

"We leave the day after tomorrow." He changed the subject. "Oh, and Niki," he continued, "I put your name on the bank account yesterday."

I smiled. "You'll see; it'll be better this way," I left it at that.

I was not in the mood to thank him. "Is your dad okay with us leaving?"

"He's good. The police have plainclothes on duty for the weekend until we get back. Just to be safe. I'm sure whoever did this has moved on."

"What about the mess?"

"I hired a crew to clean up once the police give the okay. Dad can oversee them. Best he gets back to work. He doesn't need to sit at home with too much time to think."

Clusters of people stood around to gawk at the police tape across the front door. Some whispered to each other and glanced at Thof. He shivered and shook his arms as if to shake off their stares.

"Don't worry about them; they'll go away. It will all be forgotten in a day," I said, though I didn't believe that for a minute.

"You're late. Have an eventful night?" Costa asked sarcastically when I got to work after leaving the scene. "Mom called last night. She seemed worried about you."

"Where do I start? I'm surprised you haven't heard already."

"Heard what? I've had my earphones in all morning listening to this incredible book on CD. Man, it's good. It's about this guy who—"

I cut him off. "Costa, I'm really worried about Thof. Just like your mom said, he has some shit to work out." I told him about how violent he'd been and the break-in.

"There's something else," I said.

"Gawd, there's more?"

"He was howling. I swear to God he was. It was the creepiest thing I've ever heard. His entire body changed, too. I was really afraid he was going to go over the balcony." I didn't tell him about the hair that seemed to appear spontaneously on Thof's arms.

Costa stood with his mouth open, not saying a word. Finally he sat down and picked up his coffee. "Oh…this doesn't sound good. I should call Mom and tell her she's picked up the scent."

"And now he's asked me to go to Turkey with him," I said. He as much as told me he's scared to be alone. Who could have done this?"

"Someone who has something against red wine? Well, at least we know there's nothing going on with Brielle. I was certain of that," he assured me.

"Or it's a cover."

"No, he wouldn't go to that much trouble. He doesn't think like you do." Costa winked, trying to lighten my mood. "He loves you. It's one thing you don't have to worry about."

"Well, thank God there's one thing, but I don't know if that's enough, considering."

"Niki, I have to tell you… this is the kind of stuff he was pulling that landed him in the psych ward."

"But didn't you say it was because of the drugs?"

"The drugs made what was already inside his head even worse," he said.

"There's too much going on. The tension has been so high. Something is wrong, Costa. Something big."

"I can't believe he would ever touch that stuff again. Maybe it's just stress. Maybe all the traveling is too much. Maybe the wine isn't doing as well as he's letting on."

"Well, something is going right, with all the money that's in the account," I said. "Oh, and Ugo is in the clinic. They're watching him. Thof was afraid he was having a heart attack, but it was only a panic attack. And I need to have this looked at, too." I held up my bandaged hand. The blood was beginning to soak through.

"I'm putting a sign on the door and coming with you. Then I can look in on Ugo, too."

"Thanks. I'll take you up on it. I could use a shoulder now."

"It's all yours."

Maybe Costa's the one I should be with, not Thof, I thought. Why did I always have to fall for the exotic, broken guy? Why couldn't I settle for a normal, nice one? I could have the kids he wanted, Selena could help out, and we'd live happily ever after. Who was I kidding? I wouldn't last a minute. I'd be so restless and take it out on Costa. I could see it all unraveling before my eyes.

…

With some trepidation I packed my bag for Turkey and remembered to pack a few pills of my own for the flight—a Xanax for each leg of the trip in the flying tin can; I'd been through this before—and maybe one extra in case Brielle reared her ugly head. No matter my own transgressions, it didn't change the fact that I would be devastated if I found out that Thof was up to the same things as I had been. I'd read that researchers had found a gene for monogamy and I was sure I was missing it. I tried to analyze all the what-ifs. What if bringing me along on this trip was a ruse to convince me all was on the up and up? He and Brielle would sacrifice one weekend to ensure they would have many more in the future? It would be a good plan, I thought. You're ruminating, Niki. Stop it now or I'll make you meditate. I always threatened myself with that. Usually it worked. Take some breaths. The time is now. Not tomorrow or yesterday.

After the flight, we took a boat to the Ajia Hotel, a dazzling white palace that hovered over the Bosphorus. The pristine white facade struck a blinding contrast against the crystal blue water.

"It's stunning, Thof!"

"Nineteenth century *yali*—a summer home for the Ottoman elite. I hope you like it. It's all ours."

"Like it? I'm speechless!"

"Mr. Fiomako, nice to see you again so soon," the concierge greeted him.

"*Baris.*" Thof nodded and gave a two-fingered salute as though scoutmaster of the boy scouts.

As we made our way through the vast entry, every staff

member nodded at Thof.

"Well, everyone certainly knows who you are," I commented.

"As they should, the amount of money I've spent here. They're all here at our beck and call."

Ceiling-high windows and twelve-foot-tall French doors opened to a private tiled terrace with a view of yachts and sailboats draped in thonged bodies, perfectly formed and oiled, their champagne flutes glinting in the sun. Across the strait, a coastline of miniature castles gushed baroque curlicues and finials, looking as intricate as spun sugar.

We spent the afternoon ambling along the promenade, where the water was so clear we could see the seahorses lurch along, then be swept backwards at the mercy of the current. We perused the stalls in the grand bazaar with its ornately tiled blue and white arched ceiling, stalls of colored glass lanterns, and lush fabrics. A craggy old man with a kiosk full of gramophones in various states of disrepair tinkered with a turntable. Detached horns perched on the shelves as if calling out for a disembodied turntable to give them their voices back. Old men lined the sidewalks playing backgammon at outdoor cafes.

"We really needed this." I put my hand on Thof's shoulder and sighed deeply and prayed this trip would mend all my doubts once and for all.

"A taste of what's to come for the rest of the weekend," Thof said. "And I hate to break the spell, but it's about time I catch a cab to meet Brielle. So drink some champagne and order the most expensive item on the menu for dinner for yourself, okay? Take a bubble bath. Just don't worry about anything. Promise me, babe. We have the rest of the weekend to pick up where we left off. I can't wait to get this meeting over with."

PART 2

17

*A man will renounce any pleasures you like
but he will not give up his suffering.*

— George Gurdjieff, philosopher

It seemed like a month ago that I was enjoying prawns by the waterside, anticipating the evening with Thof. Was it really last night? Hard to imagine that it was. But it was just this morning, bandaged and medicated, that I'd taken a taxi back to the villa after being released from the medical clinic. How could it possibly have happened? I wondered how much of last night I remembered correctly. Was *rape* a word I could even allow into my psyche? Images flew in and out of my mind, some in a flash, others in slow motion. It was like a dream. "Niki, remember the earrings!" Thof had yelled to me as he was being escorted out of the room, froth flying from his mouth, stretching to bite the policeman's hand that gripped his shoulder.

There was no sign there had been a struggle in the room. The rug was replaced, Thof's clothes were folded neatly on the bed, the whole place had been picked up and replenished with champagne and snacks. Between the painkillers and the pain, I questioned my recollection of the events until I saw myself in the mirror. The bandage around my head looked ridiculous, but when I pulled up my shirt, the bruises and contusions on my back had darkened to the color of an eggplant and were spreading toward the front of my rib cage like fingers wrapping around my sides. The thought of my insides looking like the pulpy spongey inside of an eggplant made me want to vomit again, but I forced it down, knowing the pain it would cause.

Another slow-motion memory—"You're going to be fine, miss," a man in a white doctor's coat said, lifting my eyelids to peer into my eyes. "But I need to get you to the hospital for observation. Are you going to want to press charges?" What had I told him?

I sat on the edge of the bed listening to the water lap at the villa. On the terrace, a bee moth hovered inside a moonflower. Its body, the size of a hummingbird, looked like a bumblebee, with alternating fuzzy stripes of gold and black. Its legs, like a moth's, were powdery white. A green furry pelt caped the back of its neck, and its wings were transparent in the middle, edged in chocolate brown like a monarch butterfly's. Its eyes twitched back and forth from the flower's intoxicating booziness to me. I sat stock still, entranced by this otherworldly creature. It dipped its curlicue antennae-like proboscis in and out of the neck of the flower. It was the most amazing thing I'd ever seen, like three different animals kludged together. It made me want to laugh, but that would've hurt too much, also. I reflexively touched my ears, feeling for the earrings Thof had given me months ago, and flashed back to the night on the rooftop when I poured them out of the bottle of wine. It came rushing back to me what he'd said last night.

"That bitch has been horning in on my territory for over a year now. She sent her thugs in to smash the wine to try to intimidate me. I'm going to kill her. Her stuff is better. She convinced me of that. I let her believe I'd team up with her. It was all a game. All lies. Asking me to partner with her, only to push me out as soon as things got up and running. How stupid did she think I was? I saw right through it. Her time is short now. We're going to tell her 'Yes, we're in,' you and me, then we cut her throat. We'll have enough of her pharm to keep us going for a year. That will give us enough time to figure out her recipe. We up our prices to match hers. Fuck the wine. The wine is the carrier pigeon; the pills are the message, baby. It's all in the bottle. One case of wine is now worth fifty K. A private little Pandora's box can be yours for a tidy sum."

It meant that Thof had been working with Brielle for at least a year. Had he even been working with her when we first met? And the werefox episodes he had, were they all a result of her drugs? The earrings had gotten into the bottle the same way he got the pills into them! This was such a sudden dump of realizations, it made me woozy.

The bee moth vanished. I lowered my hand and touched Thof's neatly folded shirt beside me on the bed. I inhaled his scent from it, earthy and musky, felt the cool marble floor under my feet, the silky duvet cover under my legs, and the salty breeze on my skin. Then I felt the wallet in Thof's pants.

I covered the bed with its contents like a game of solitaire. Driver's license, credit cards, health insurance card, government-issued ID, gym membership cards for all over Asia, our coin, rectangular pieces of black foil in a plastic sleeve for re-sealing bottles, and cash—ten thousand dollars in cash, and a cashier's check made out to Koraki for half a million dollars, signed by Brielle!

Holy shit. Thoughts raced through my head with a blinding whir. The check made out to the wine bar explained the extra zeros on the bank statements. This has been going on for years, I thought. No wonder he didn't want me to have access to the bank account.

I'd come so far, geographically and emotionally since leaving Jin. I was young and easily manipulated then, yet here I was, duped again. When would I ever learn?

My heart pounded in my throat in spite of the pain meds,

which made me feel like a marshmallow. Then my mind clicked off and my body took over. I pocketed the coin, nine thousand dollars plus a few more odd notes, and the cashier's check. I shoved everything else back into Thof's wallet, threw my things into my bag, and called a taxi for the airport in spite of the doctor's order that I stay at least another day before flying back.

The same time my hand turned the doorknob, someone started banging from the other side.

Oh, fuck, my head. "Stop!" I pleaded to whoever was doing it and opened the door.

"Oh my God… your head…" Costa tried to cover his shock as we stood face to face in the doorway. He looked like he was about to cry.

"Try being inside it," I said. "And that's the least of it—a broken rib and bruised spleen, too. The doctor said I wasn't supposed to fly yet, but I want to get back so badly. Wait, what are you doing here? I'm really out of it. How did you find me?"

"Thof called me last night. He was going a mile a minute. Insanely agitated."

"I know! I was here. He was psychotic."

"He told me everything," Costa said. "His plan for Brielle, what he's been up to all this time, and that he knew about us. I took the first flight I could get because I was scared of what he would do to you. I was right. Oh, shit. I'm so, so sorry. I should have known. I should have done something long ago. Can you ever forgive me?" He took me into his arms.

"Ow! Stop!" I cried. "I'm going home, Costa." I couldn't begin to process what he was saying, much less what Thof had done to me.

"I know, Nik. Let's go."

"No, I mean *home* home. I'm going back to the States. I just have a few loose ends to tie up first."

I played out the entire story (except for the money I'd taken) to Costa on the flight back to Nafplio.

"It's crazier than I ever could have imagined. Not only using drugs but running them? Completely insane. I mean, honestly, I'm really having a hard time believing it. It's like I've been living in a movie. I'm done, Costa. Please don't hold it against me. I guess I had this coming," I said.

"Are you kidding? I don't blame you. Knowing Thof for as long as I have, I should've seen the signs. I should've questioned him. You don't deserve this. No one does," he told me.

Then he told me about the phone call Thof had made to him from the villa.

…

The LSD originated in Istanbul, where cases of wine from Thof's father were shipped ahead of Thof, to Tarlabasi, where he'd meet the drug drop in a different back alley each trip.

"That's so close to where we stayed. We passed right by it," I said—the makeshift tents, and sandaled men draped in kaftans calling out from their fluttering plastic-roofed stalls late into the night. *Knives! Propane! Sheep heads!* It's a poor neighborhood where the buildings are crumbling, garbage is strewn in the gutters, and gang members patrol, yet it's less than a five-minute walk to the glitzy markets and boutiques.

Costa continued with his story.

Thof relied on a local scout, who knew every dark corner tucked away in plain sight—a rug seller's storage room, a tailor's fitting closet, a cook's cold room. In his hideaway, behind a curtain or makeshift plywood panel, he performed the drill. Unseen by anyone, it appeared that Thof had merely picked up a case of wine. The routine took a minute and required only an extension cord to power a heat gun. The only sound was the cheery pop of a cork and the whispering whir of the gun. The tiny pills were in plastic shrink-wrapped tubes, which the scout had prepared. Thof took a swallow of wine out of one bottle to make room for the small tube, which displaced the wine by only half an inch, dropped it into the bottle, recorked it, slipped the foil over the neck, and blasted it with the heat gun. He handed off the case to his scout and dropped the heat gun in a dumpster somewhere along the way. There was one bottle of wine in the case that was now worth $50K. The scout shipped the case to Thof's destination, usually somewhere in Asia, where it would be waiting at his hotel. The bottle was distinguished only by a slightly lighter colored foil. If you weren't examining the bottles, you would never know. In fact, even when customs had examined them, they went undetected. The wine was excellent, but brought in pennies compared to the drugs. The bottom line made his father very proud.

"You think Ugo had no clue? I find that hard to believe," I said.

"I'm not sure about that. A man of so few words. Hard to know what's going on in that head. Anyway, the morning Thof ran into us at the resort in Cesme?"

"Yes?"

"He wasn't meeting a grower; he was actually meeting Brielle."

"I knew it."

"No, not what you're thinking. True, he'd been meeting her at the start of all of his trips, but it was purely business," Costa told me and continued the story.

Thof and Brielle updated each other on their projects; she, developing the perfect chemical concoction to deliver a high never known before; he, looking for new connections to buy his spiked cases of wine. They brainstormed and strategized, knowing there was no one else either could trust with their secrets. Thof sampled her wares and reported back to her. Brielle introduced him to elite acquaintances she'd made as she traveled around the globe as a pharmaceutical rep for one of the largest companies in the world. She also introduced him to the lowest of low drug suppliers from whom he could buy drugs to drop into his wine.

"They were both using each other. Like the small fish that attaches to a shark's underbelly to eat its parasites—the fish gets nourishment, the shark gets groomed," Costa commented.

"Talk about a shark."

"Deep down I think Thof knew he was sinking into an abyss again. I'm sure that's why he called me. He sounded high as a kite, but also desperate for help."

"Which explains his wildly erratic swings," I said, implying both his moods and his fists.

For once the flight didn't scare me half to death, and before I knew it, we had landed.

Costa helped me up the stairs to the apartment. I was completely drained, but also felt a tinge of excitement. Or was it fear? Sometimes it was hard to tell the difference. He offered to stay, but I needed time alone to be quiet and to think.

...

"Poor Minky," I cooed to the cat. "It's just you and me now. What am I going to do with you?"

I couldn't abandon her in the apartment, alone for who knew how long. Selena! Costa's mother would be perfect. She could add Minky to her collection of lazy sun-worshiping cats. And it would be a good excuse to see her again, one last time. I'd arrange a trip with Costa.

But first, I had some bank business to attend to. I had to be prepared for the hassle I was sure the bank would give me when I presented a half million dollar cashier's check. Not only was I a woman (which made a difference in this provincial town), but my name was put on the account only last week—auspicious timing for me, but bound to look fishy. For the next two days, I chewed over what I was about to do a thousand times—abscond with half a million dollars of drug money and the cash from Thof's pocket. I couldn't help but think that maybe he had planned to spend it on an engagement ring, but I put that thought out of my head fast. I didn't want to dwell on anything that might make me change my mind. Thof had gone over the edge—legally and mentally. I couldn't fix either one and didn't expect anyone else could,

either, at least not any time in the near future. He had seriously checked out. Now it was my turn—right out of Nafplio
before Brielle got wind of the missing money. I figured I had
only a few days before she'd start to wonder why Thof wasn't
getting back to her about her business proposition. And who
knew how long it would be until Thof came back—if he did
at all? I wasn't about to try to communicate with officials in
Turkey to try to find out his status. I couldn't have any connection to him. I had to disappear. Dematerialize. I had to start
moving my body. Force myself into a hot shower. Under
normal circumstances I would be nursing my wounds in bed
for another week, but I sensed the clock ticking, time pressing
down on me.

The bank was bound to put a hold on the check, not only
because they didn't know me, but because no bank in the area
would have that kind of cash on hand. It would have to be
transferred in. I needed to start the process now, so by the
time I got back from Selena's the money would be ready. But
then how would I get the money out of the country? I couldn't
simply put it in my wallet.

"How am I going to get a wad like that out of the country,
Minky? In a cat carrier? Crazy. It will come. It will come." I
talked to the cat, trying to convince myself it would all work
out. "One thing at a time, Mink."

The day was overcast, but the haze was certain to burn off by midday. It was a relief. It kept me calm, like a heavy blanket. I unwrapped my bandaged head. I couldn't imagine how bandages could help a concussion. A small Band-Aid would do to cover the stitches, and a scarf would hide the shaved spot. I twisted the ends together on top of my head and tucked them in to secure it, leaving my bangs loose around my face. I chose a dark blue dress that I never wore because it was just a little too big, and a thin cardigan over it. I wanted the perfect balance of conservative and businesslike, yet naive and innocent.

"Pack your bags, Ms. Minky," I told her. "When I get back from the bank we're going on a trip. You're going to make some new friends." Minky looked at me quizzically, cocking her head.

There was a line at the bank. I counted and recounted the people. Eight ahead of me gave me too much time to get nervous. I reminded myself to breathe from my belly, making my exhalations longer than my inhalations. When that didn't help, I pinched the fleshy space between my thumb and forefinger hard until it left a mark on my skin and the pain was searing. Anything to take my mind off what I was about to attempt.

The woman in front of me chewed her gum like a cow

chewing its cud. I wanted to tell her how ugly it was, not to mention how irritating the wet smacking sound was. And she should really stand up straight, too. She'd look five years younger, if only she'd pull her shoulders back and suck her stomach in.

The man behind me was practically up against my back. Why must people get so close? It's not going to make the line go any faster. I called them PSI, personal space invaders. I took half a step forward while leaving one foot a half step behind. Sensing my forward movement, the PSI stepped forward, bumping into me as I lowered the heel of my back foot right onto his. It got them every time. He jumped back and apologized. My foot remained half a step back as a warning.

Of the three bank tellers, there were two women and one man. I definitely wanted the man. I could play him, if needed, more easily than a woman. It was timing out perfectly as I got to the front of the line and the customer at the man's station turned to leave. I stepped forward, but the customer turned back to the teller. Damn. I stepped back in line, backing into the man behind me once again. One of the women tellers called me up.

"Miss. Next," she called out, waving me up.

"Oh, shoot. I can't find my bank card," I stammered. "Sorry, sorry," I said to the PSI in line behind me. "You go ahead." I fumbled in my bag, sending curses to the customer at the man's station. Finally he finished.

"Sorry about that," I smiled at the teller as I stepped up to his window. "I thought I forgot the check I came here to cash, but it was in my bag the whole time. Of course." I pushed the half million dollar cashier's check with Brielle's signature on it along with my ID through the bulletproof slot that separated us.

He did a double take when he saw the check, trying hard to conceal his surprise. "Excuse me for a moment. I'll have to okay this with the manager," he told me.

Breathe. Be cool.

The teller returned with the manager by his side. "Hello…" the manager said, then paused and looked at my ID to find my name. "Niki. Have you been banking with us for long?"

"Yes. Well, actually my husband has—Theodore Fiomako—for about five years now."

"I see that." The manager looked at the check again, as though searching for answers on it he may have missed. "Is Theodore available?"

"No, he's out of the country on business. It's why he recently added my name to the account. He's traveling more and more while I'm running the business for him here in town." I fiddled with my scarf as I felt the glass barrier between us getting thicker. Was I losing him?

"It's highly irregular to cash a check of this amount with no history of you banking with us," Mr. Manager said. He had a boyish look, but was working on a five-o-clock shadow. A nice combination, I thought. I bet he was a surfer. His hair was tousled, as though he'd just woken up from a nap. His teeth were perfectly white, emphasizing his dimples.

"Yes, of course. I understand. It was a last-minute trip. He had to leave quickly. We didn't have time to come in and make the introductions. He knew the check would be coming in while he was gone, which is why he requested a cashier's check from his vendor. Hoping, of course, that you would understand this one time." I smiled and played with my earring. I'd read that men are distracted by dangly, shiny objects. If you want to fluster them a bit, play with your hoops and watch their eyes glaze over.

I swirled some energy around myself. I didn't expect that it would have any effect, especially with the one-inch-thick, bulletproof glass between me and the boyish bankers. I breathed my energy down the front of myself and up my back a few times, swirling it faster and faster until I felt my body getting lighter and lifting off the floor. Just like Thof had taught me. The pressure from the weight of my body was gone from the soles of my feet. I felt a pulsing aura emanating from my entire body. The glass barrier glowed as if the sun had just broken through the clouds, brightening up the room. Both men looked up from their huddled whispering over the check. I smiled at them and winked. Oh my gawd, I couldn't believe I'd done that. They both smiled back at me.

The tousle-haired manager buzzed himself out from behind the thick glass and met me on my side. The teller glared at him for leaving him behind while the manager put his hand on my shoulder.

"Mrs. Fiomako," the manager started. "I didn't know you and Mr. Fiomako had gotten married."

"Yes, it was surprise to everyone, but mostly me. Just last week when we took a little weekend on the Bosphorus." I hadn't planned on the conversation going this far. "We did it right then and there. No planning. No stress. Poof! and it was done. I suppose that's another reason he added my name to the account. He had the wedding up his sleeve the entire time."

"You must be very happy," the manager squeezed my shoulder. "Let me see what I can do for you about this check. We don't have that kind of cash on hand. I'll have to order it. It may take some time."

"I was expecting that. But not too much time, I hope. Mr. Fiomako is needing it before the end of the week for some private investing. I'm meeting him in Thailand, where he's finishing up some wine business, then we're going to Bali on our honeymoon." I played with my scarf again and pushed a little energy toward the manager.

"Is it cold in here?" the manager asked, rubbing his arms. "Just a little. Yes." I winked at him again.

"I'll call you by tomorrow and let you know when you can expect the cash, Niki. I mean Mrs. Fiomako," he stammered.

"Please call me Niki," I touched his arm and saw the glow of sweat on his forehead, in spite of the chill. I handed him my phone number. "Leave a message if I don't pick up. I'm planning on visiting a friend out of town in the next day or so."

Outside the bank and around the corner I did a little happy

dance, but quickly composed myself. You're not out of the gate yet, I reminded myself.

...

I called Costa to arrange a trip to Selena's. I didn't dare tell him what I was up to. He'd surely try to talk me out of it, being forever the good guy. Was there an integrity gene? Seemed like I was missing that one, too. If I could pull this off, I'd be set to do whatever I could dream of. Go anywhere. I'd wait until I was settled in my new home, wherever that might be, before telling Costa what I'd done. Now, I had three days to figure out how to get the cash out of the country.

As usual, I blabbed nonstop the entire drive to Selena's. Apparently manic. Costa let me go on and on with my rant over what had become of my life. As we pulled into the gravel lane, the sight of Selena waiting outside to greet us made a lump rise in my throat. I took a deep breath, and as her arms reached out to me, my emotions surged. She hugged me tight, then the dam broke. Sobs burst out of me like candy from a piñata. Just when I thought there were none left, another clobber and more sobs burst forth.

"Niki, Niki, my poppet, what's the matter?" Selena kept a tight hold on me.

"I'm sorry. Oh my gawd, I'm sorry," I gulped. "I wasn't expecting this." I tried to laugh to cover up my crying, but snorted instead.

"Now that was funny," Costa chuckled, joining in the embrace. "I wondered when it would come out. You were gushing at such a pace the entire drive."

"*Éla, Éla.*" Selena led me inside. *Come, come.* "What on earth has happened?"

"Wait, I almost forgot." I went back to the Jeep and retrieved a cardboard box from the floor and handed it to Selena.

"What's this?" she asked as the box wobbled and a meow came from inside. Selena's face lit up, and a huge grin spread across her face like a child about to receive a giant lollipop.

"Her name's Minky," I said as a furry paw poked out of the gap between the closed flaps. Selena opened the lid and Minky bounded out, right up onto her shoulder.

"You're an instant hit," Costa said.

"I'm afraid she needs a home," I said. "I hope you have room."

"Look around you!" Selena extended her arm toward the vista of olive trees and terraced hillsides. "But why?"

"We have the whole evening for that. And believe me, it will take all that time to explain," Costa said. "We'll put our stuff away first and join you in a minute."

"I need a cleanup after that drive and now my face is puffy. Great," I said.

"I'll pour the grappa," Selena offered.

"That should hit the spot. Thank you," I accepted.

"Shit, that was crazy," I said to Costa once inside his room. "One look at your mom and it all came bursting out."

"You absolutely needed it, Nik. And I'm sure there's more to come." He handed me a cool, wet towel.

...

We spent the evening drinking, eating, and explaining to Selena all that happened—rehashing everything from my initial suspicions of Koraki's ever-increasing bank balance and Brielle's mysterious appearances to the recent events in the villa that gave me the contusions on my body and stitches on my scalp.

I felt like I was betraying Selena and Costa by not telling them about my plans for the money and wondered if Selena sensed I wasn't telling them the entire story.

"What will you do now?" Selena asked.

"I've been over it a hundred times, and I decided it's time to go back to the States. Meditate. Write. Maybe go on a retreat for a month. Try to get perspective on all that's happened. I've always wanted to go to the Zen center near Muir Beach in

California. The redwoods are fantastic and it's so close to the water. I can smell it now. In fact, it reminds me of Nafplio with the cliffs and ocean. I guess I'll always be drawn to that, like it's in my blood."

"That and exotic men," Costa retorted with a sly grin.

"Ouch! Rub salt in a wound why don't you?" I winked.

"Sorry. I couldn't help it. It sounds perfect. We'll be waiting to hear who the next one is, though," Costa said.

"Ignore him, Niki." Selena came to my rescue. "What comes to you will be exactly what is supposed to, at the exact moment it should. I sense that your soul spirit is guiding you to exactly the right spot. Trust it."

"Soul spirit? Yeah, I was into that when Thof and I first met. Needless to say I've let it go by the wayside."

A coyote's bark rang out in the distance like a gargling laugh. *Woo-oo-wow. Yip yip.* "Oh, shit. That gives me goose bumps," I said.

"It's a greeting call," Selena explained. "Others will answer soon."

"I started having dreams about a pack of fox, my pack, when I first got to Nafplio. It's been a long time since I've had one of them."

"Our coyote friends couldn't have timed it more perfectly," Selena said. "Sometimes the synchronicity even surprises me! A new pack is calling you, Niki. Reconnect to it."

I thought of the money again. Were my injuries forward payment for it? If Selena was right, I'd better take the money and run. Have faith it would all fall into place.

"What are you thinking?" Selena asked.

"Oh, just wondering if I'd do it all over again. I'd have to say that I would." I nudged Costa's foot under the table.

Minky stretched out on a slab of slate and batted at a grass-hopper.

"Looks like she's going to fit right in," Selena said. "Just like you have, Niki. I'll miss you and will be thinking of you."

My mind wandered nervously again. Would the bank really hand the money over to me? It was almost too good to be true. Would I be able to keep my cool if they questioned me further? Even if it all went off without a hitch, I still had to get the cash out of the country.

"Earth to Niki," Costa said.

"Oh, sorry. It must be the grappa gone to my head. How 'bout another?" I asked.

"That's the spirit; it will do you good," Selena said, pouring another round. "Now tell me, Niki, are you set with money? I hope Thof has at least provided for you, given all the work you've done for him at the bar, not to mention the abuse."

I stared, one silent beat too long, thinking about everything Thof had told me about how he smuggled the drugs out in the wine bottles. Selena and Costa waited, staring back at me.

"It's the strangest thing… I have this feeling," I started, ignoring Selena's inquiry. "Like he's calling me. I mean literally on the phone. As though he's back at work and calling home to check in. I can't brush it off. Like after your dog dies and you still expect him to come trotting around the corner. You listen for the sound of his nails on the floor and the jingle of his collar. It's so ingrained."

"What would you do if he did? I mean, not that he would ever be allowed to from a Turkish jail cell," Costa asked. "Gawd, the thought of him in there."

"I don't want to think about it. I'd be scared and sad at the same time if he called. Scared for my safety and sad for us, in spite of it all. For the loss of the gorgeous man I fell in love with." I reached across the table and squeezed Costa's hand and gave him a knowing look. It meant, I love you too, but we both know it's not sustainable. He squeezed my hand back.

"Okay, call me crazy, but I just have to call home and check the machine." I pushed my chair away from the table and headed to the kitchen, where the phone sat on the counter, convenient for Selena, who spent most of her time there cooking, canning, and baking.

The solution had come to me. I'd put the money into wine bottles the same way Thof got my earrings in the bottle.

Coyote yip-howls rose up again, but this time from a large group and the barks turned into screams.

My hand trembled as I dialed the number to our phone at the apartment. Where was this urge to call home coming from? I hoped it was nothing, yet couldn't get over the strong pull of my intuition. The phone rang and rang, then an odd click, then the ringing continued. When the answering machine didn't pick up, I knew it was because someone was leaving a message at that very moment. I broke into a cold sweat, hung up, and poured myself a glass of water from the kitchen sink. Holy fuck. Someone was calling.

There's no way it could be Thof. Literally impossible. Was I afraid it was a ghost or something? Niki, get a hold of yourself! It's probably just Ugo. Yes, that was surely it. I convinced myself of it and picked up the phone and dialed again. This time the machine picked up. I dialed in my code to retrieve any messages and took another gulp of water.

"You have. Two. Messages," the machine announced. "Message. Number one," it said in its choppy robotic voice. "Message sent today. At five. Fifty. Two."

I glanced at my watch: 5:53.

"Thof. Brielle here. Why have I not heard from you?"

"Message complete," the machine whined. "To save message. Press—"

I hung up the phone and stared out the kitchen window. On the terrace, Selena and Costa clinked glasses under the grape-draped arbor and threw back their shots of grappa. The sky was turning orange-pink as the sun began its hazy slow descent beyond the olive trees and slatey terraces. Scores of dragonflies buzzed each other in silent, hypnotic battles, their wings glinting in the angular rays of light.

Brielle was worse than any ghost I could conjure. She was smart, rich, fearless, and knocked it out of the park with her looks. Every woman's bane. According to Thof's tirade the night in Istanbul before the police dragged him away, she had been double-crossing him the entire time, planning to dethrone him from his territory. Her plan at dinner had been to wait until he agreed to team up with her, then to seal the deal. She told him she was going to enable him to double his earnings. But what did she have planned then? Have him killed? Turn him in? Bungle his jobs? I still didn't understand how Thof was on to her. I guess I'll never find out. But Brielle was still under the assumption that Thof was under her spell, and she had no intention of letting that money get away. It was all part of her ploy to get him to trust her. For Christ's sake, her name meant warrior of God! She sure fit the bill.

In my head, I ran through the supplies I needed for the job: shrink-wrap tubes, heat gun, neck foils, wine key. Exactly the same tools Thof used to get the drugs into his bottles. I would do the same with the money. I could fit all the tools except the heat gun in the pockets of my jeans if I had to. How much easier could it get than that? But I'd need to call in an order to Ugo—a big one since I had no idea how many bottles I'd need. I had to be sure my bases were covered. I'd figure out exactly how many I needed later and tell him I'd made a mistake if I needed to—that I'd somehow left off a zero from Thof's order. He'd make a show of irritation at having to redo the paperwork, but would be giddily gloating to himself while making plans for the extra income. I knew him too well. He'd be overjoyed for the huge order.

Brielle was my only wild card now. How long would it take her to realize Thof was incommunicado? How long before she came looking for him and followed her nose to me? I had to get out of here.

But wait! There were two messages! I'd almost forgotten. I quickly redialed. It cannot get any worse than this.

"You have. One. Message," the machine announced.

"Yeah, yeah. Hurry it up," I caught myself saying out loud.

"Message sent yesterday. At four. forty. five. p.m."

"Hello, Mrs. Fiomako… uh… Niki. This is Sami, the manager, from Piraeus Bank. Something has come up. Can you please give me a call?"

No No No No No, I screamed in my head. I leaned over the sink and put my face in my hands, blinking hard and fast, then started pacing back and forth like a caged animal.

Pull it together, Niki! Call Ugo and get this deal moving!

I dialed Ugo at the shop as Costa yelled from the terrace. "Niki! What are you doing in there? Are you okay? Bring another bottle."

"Coming!"

"*Kaló apógevma, Ugozuzzo*," Ugo answered gruffly on the second ring. *Good afternoon.* I never could tell when he was speaking Greek or English, or a combination of both. When I had asked Thof what *Ugozuzzo* meant, a word I couldn't find in any Greek dictionary, he explained that Ugo was saying Ugo's Ouzo, the name of the shop. It attracted tourists who were interested in kitschy bottles of ouzo to take home with them.

"*Chaírete*," I formally responded—*Hello*—momentarily forgetting my predicament, automatically uncomfortable with the man who never missed an opportunity to patronize me.

Silence on the other end. I had to pull myself together. "Uh, sorry for the late call, but Thof has flown off to Thailand. I'm meeting him there in a few days. Uh… he asked me to let you know he has a large order he needs shipped out tomorrow."

"*Nai*," Ugo managed. *Yes.*

"I'll be home in the morning to help you with it." I wondered what I was setting myself up for.

"*Nai*," Ugo farted out again. The man was a dolt.

"Seventy cases of the usual mix." I took a stab at a quantity. It was so unrehearsed I was impressed with myself as it spilled off my tongue. "Destination, Thailand. I'll bring the details when I get intomorrow."

"*Nai, kalos.*" *Yes, okay.*

"Ciao!" I managed cheerily, but I slammed the phone down. Less is more was always my motto. Shut up and hang up.

I splashed my face with water from the kitchen sink and rummaged through the sideboard for another bottle of grappa. Keep it together, Niki; just keep it together.

"Well? Any message? I thought I heard you talking to someone," Costa said when I got outside.

"No. I mean yes, but just to tell Ugo about the order he's putting together for the Thai shipment. I'd forgotten about it. I suppose I should help him with it tomorrow. It's so big and he'll be expecting Thof." As the words tumbled out, I realized I'd given myself the perfect excuse to leave early. God knows I didn't want to leave the cocoon-like safety of Selena's house, but I had to.

"That must make him happy. His wine sales are really picking up. But what about Thof?" Selena asked. "Ugo deserves to know what happened. He'll find out sooner or later anyway."

"Costa said he'd tell him, but I think I'll do it. One last attempt at communication."

"He'll be heartbroken," Costa said.

"You might be surprised," Selena said. "He's always been waiting for the other shoe to drop. They'll work through it, though, like they have many times before."

"It doesn't help that Ugo and I never hit it off. I don't know what the man has against me."

"He's just overly protective since Thof's mother passed away," Selena said. "How many years has it been? He denies it, but that's what it is. All he sees is a pretty young American swooping into town for a good time. He doesn't trust and doesn't bother to give you a chance. Typical." Selena snorted a knowing laugh.

"Men," I said.

"Men," Costa added.

"Seriously, men," I said.

"Oy, I think we've hit a wall," Costa said.

"Then let's hit the hay," Selena said in a rare play on

words—a tipsy departure from her usual serious timbre.

The evening had grown chilly. Fall was coming. I left the doors open so the cold air and Minky could meander in and out, and climbed under the down comforter with Costa. We held each other sweetly, both knowing it would be the last time.

"Are you sure you're okay with telling Ugo? I'll do it if you don't feel up to it," Costa spoke quietly in the dark.

"I'm okay. It's the least I can do," I assured him. I had no intention of saying a word to Ugo. By the time he found out about Thof's arrest I'd be long gone—the wine shipment redirected to the U.S. I did feel bad about essentially stealing Ugo's wine, and decided that I would repay him, anonymously, when the time came.

"I think it'd be better if I drove back tomorrow myself. Can I take the Jeep? Can we say our goodbyes here?"

"Sure. I was thinking the same thing."

I could feel his warm breath on my ear.

"I'll make an excuse to stay here with Selena and drive in with her later in the week."

I pulled him tighter, melancholic. Everything was going to start moving fast now. I could feel it.

"I hate goodbyes," I whispered, turning my face toward his. "This will make it more bearable. I'll be able to get my stuff together back in Nafplio and tie up loose ends at the bar before leaving without wondering if you're going to jump me in the middle of the night." I tried to lighten the mood, forcing a laugh, hoping I hadn't been too crass. I was hugely relieved I'd be able to work through the night at the wine bar, filling the bottles with cash, without worrying that he might have a sleepless night and wander in at three in the morning. I wouldn't have to be looking over my shoulder.

My mind raced and my body buzzed as I lay there, afraid the energy coursing off me would keep Costa awake. Among other things, it occurred to me: Why should I repay Ugo? Thof would get out of jail and return home eventually. He was sure to have money stashed in places I didn't know. Let him repay

Ugo. And I couldn't shake the thought that Brielle would very soon be on my tail.

I was going to go out of my mind if I stayed in bed one minute longer. As soon as Costa's breathing deepened and steadied, his hand loosening its hold on mine, I snuck out. I quietly gathered the few items I'd brought along, shoved them into my duffel bag, and lifted Costa's keys out of his back pocket. What a gorgeous back pocket, I thought… last chance. My eyes welled up at the thought of never seeing him or Selena again. I felt a hole in my chest. I had a fleeting vision of crawling back into bed and pretending none of this happened.

Minky was sitting outside the front door, preening in the moonlight. "A nice night for driving," I told her. "Bye-bye, babe," I said and gave her a pat on the head.

19

The trip from Peristeria back to Nafplio was an easy shot. West on A8, then south on the E65—just a two-hour drive, 126 kilometers, through ragged, stabbing terrain. About halfway I decided to take the scenic route though, cutting due south on the E10, which would, after a few harrowing switchbacks and miles and miles of olive groves, spit me out at the water's edge in Nafplio. It would make the trip thirty minutes longer, but I couldn't leave without one last magnificent view of the blue-green Saronic Gulf glinting against the moon.

I had no problem staying awake for the drive, that's for sure, and I didn't even want coffee to keep me company. Instead I did calculations in my head, trying to figure out how many hundred-dollar notes (the largest denomination in print) there are in half a million dollars. Math was never my strong suit, so it took a few tries of tapping out zeros on the steering wheel with my fingers to make sure I got it right. Five thousand bills! Shit, that was going to be a lot of bottles. Thof would only alter one bottle per case. It kept his odds much better if he was ever caught or somehow lost a case along the way. I was going to have to use more bottles per case, otherwise it would be such a large order that Ugo would ask questions. I couldn't risk the order looking too extraordinary.

How many rolled bills could even fit in the neck of a bottle? Would the heat-shrink tube be strong enough to compress the roll while keeping it watertight too? And where in the hell was I going to buy heat-shrink tubing? That was one detail Thof left out in his wild rant. A hardware store would look suspicious, me being a woman, and could be traced. I'd have to order it by phone. If I did that the moment I got home, it would be early enough to ship the same day. Great! Okay, but how much to buy? Oh my gawd. What am I going to forget?

I was glad for the devilish switchbacks, which forced me to drive slowly and concentrate; otherwise I'd be driving way too fast, on autopilot, with no awareness of where I even was. I knew that feeling—arriving somewhere only to wonder how I'd gotten there. What route did I take? Did I go through any red lights?

Back to more math and tapping the steering wheel. If I could fit twenty-five bills in a bottle, I would need 200 bottles. If every single bottle in the case had money in it, that would be seventeen cases. In the wine business (in Thof's wine business, that is), seventeen cases was a small shipment, but there was no way I could risk opening and stuffing every single bottle in every case.

Loading four bottles per case would take fifty cases (a nice wine sale). Two bottles per case, 100 cases, would be a beautiful sale in Ugo's eyes. This was starting to sound like the perfect bowl of porridge. What was the perfect scenario for Ugo? What would make him very happy and keep him imagining that Thof must be working very hard? Wherever that might be. Did Ugo even wonder? Or did he only care about the bottom line? That was not for me to worry over. Let the man have a few more days of peace.

So 100 cases. Settled. Sounded like a nice number. Twelve hundred bottles. That would be almost a $50,000.00 sale for Ugo. An entire year's earnings!

With no traffic this early in the morning the air was fresh.

None of the hot, sticky dust to cling to me that the afternoon commuters kicked up. The smell of the ocean was strong now, so home was close by. *Home*, I thought, surprised at how easily that word came. No more.

I forced myself to go over the plan again and again and again. I couldn't afford to get lazy or miss something. I'd arrive in Nafplio by 1:00 a.m. and have to hit the ground running. The town would be deserted, the tourist season finally over. The locals were taking their own well-deserved, though short-lived vacations, retreating into the quiet of their homes early in the evenings. In only a few weeks, the holiday season would start with a new influx of travelers.

Once back in Nafplio, I'd first have to create the paper-work. I'd seen Thof fill it out a million times and give it to his father to put orders together: whites, reds, sweet Malagousia, and of course retsina. Then I'd have to pull the bottles, check them off the purchase list, add a packing list to each case, put a shipping label on the box, and call DHL for a pickup. How many times had I even done it myself when the bar was slow and Ugo wasn't available? No problem, Niki. Easy-peasy. The only difference was that this time it would be at 1:00 in the morning, and there would be 100 cases, not seventeen. I'd have my work cut out for me, but I kept telling myself I was used to wrestling cases of wine up and down ladders and hand-trucking them half a block from the shop to the wine bar. This shouldn't be any different.

By the time Ugo came around to open his shop later in the day, the cases would already be in the bar, stacked, labeled, presumably ready a day early. I'd tell him I'd had a terribly sleepless night and decided to get up and do something instead of worrying my pretty little head over poor Thof and his far-flung travels. I'd assure him the shipment would be picked up the following day as usual. All I had to do was tape the cases shut. That would give me overnight to apply the new labels over the Thailand-addressed labels and insert the money into the bottles.

I went through every step in my head, from uncorking to foiling, while keeping one eye on the Jeep's clock blinking off the digital seconds. Two hundred bottles to manipulate. About one minute each. That was less than four hours. Of course I would need breaks and might mess up a few bottles and have to redo them. Even if it took twice the time, it'd be a walk in the park! My self-talk was getting louder and louder. I eased the Jeep over onto the shoulder and rifled through my bag to find a pen and paper. I had to get this out of my head and down on paper. Ugo would be thrilled to not have to do the heavy lifting and would invite his friends into his shop for a round (or three) on the house, bragging about his forthcoming windfall. He'd not venture out again after his afternoon siesta, as he often slept off his midday happy hour through the night. I'd be assured a night to work with no interruptions.

I'd even have time for a catnap when I was done if I could calm down. I'd have to try; otherwise I'd not only look like shit when I went to the bank, but worse, I'd be a total nut case. The bank didn't open until 10:00, so I'd have more than enough time to close my eyes for a few minutes. Just needed to stay focused, calm, and hydrated. Please, God, don't let there be a problem. In the meantime, should I return the call from the bank? What did he say his name was? Maybe I should show up and tell him I was away and didn't get his message. What could he possibly want? Why couldn't he have left a message explaining what he needed? Did Brielle stop payment? Can you do that with a cashier's check? Maybe the bank couldn't obtain the cash? The police would be there waiting for me? There was so much I couldn't foresee. So much I didn't even know to question until the moment was upon me. I just had to keep moving.

To save my wrist from all the twisting out of corks, and to get the job done faster, I'd use the mounted cork puller to open the bottles, then pound the corks back in. But I couldn't use the heel of my hand on 200 bottles. I'd try to remember to grab a rubber mallet from the tool kit. I knew from experience that it was easier to recork a bottle by turning the cork upside down. It was slightly narrower at the bottom and went most of the way back in with an easy push. Of course the exposed end would be stained red from having been inside the bottle, but what did I care? It would be covered with a new foil. If screened, no one would ever know.

I added it all to the list and kept writing. I could afford another ten minutes pulled off the road. This morning would be the easy part—getting the cases to the wine bar. I'd done it many times over the last year. This afternoon would be the real test. I'd have to play Ugo just right and keep my cool, as though it was a normal day. I'd pack the rest of my clothes and have a few practice runs with test bottles when I got back from the bank. Tomorrow—fly out. The wine would actually arrive ahead of me.

I wrote down the timeline:

TODAY

- 1 a.m. — arrive home
- Wine bar: place order for heat-shrink tubing from 24-hour electrical hardware store in Athens. Guarantee same day delivery!!
- Clear space for cases at wine bar/schedule DHL pickup
- Move Jeep to Ugo's shop/create order in computer/ pull bottles
- Grab heat gun
- 5 a.m. — print both real and fake shipping labels/ load Jeep
- Unload cases at wine bar
- 6 a.m. — call LA wine storage to reserve space and schedule delivery
- Address cases with Thai shipping labels
- 6:20 a.m. — home/shower
- 9 a.m. — nap!!!
- Track shrink-wrap delivery

- Leave for bank to arrive by 10 a.m.
- 11 a.m. — home: NO GLITCHES ALLOWED
- Day to kill
- Stay calm!
- Putter at wine bar until Ugo checks in/practice on a few bottles in apartment/pack
- Buy plane ticket to LA for following day
- Back to wine bar to do the wine bottles!!

TOMORROW
- 6 a.m. — Shower/dress
- Load Jeep with luggage/meet DHL at bar for pickup
- Jeep to airport/long-term parking lot/drop the keys in the mail to Costa

I pulled back onto the highway: 12:45 a.m.

...

How different it was pulling into Nafplio this chilly fall morning from what it was almost three years ago, the summer I met Thof. Then, the narrow, winding streets and alleys, scented with bougainvillea, were lit up and crowded with partiers at 1:00 in the morning. Music and shouts of hawkers flowed from every open door. Energy spun like invisible vortexes that night on his boat. What a whirlwind it had been. I was amazed at the life changes I'd made in such a short time.

Now, except for the sound of the Jeep's tires crunching gravel on the cobblestones, Nafplio was shuttered and silent as I pulled up to Koraki. My keys jangled harshly in the stillness. First item on my list: heat-shrink tubing. I wanted to make the call from the wine bar so it wouldn't show up on Ugo's phone bill. The least I could do was bury the call in the bar's bill.

In the packing and supply section of the giant hardware supplier's catalog, I found what I hoped and prayed would work. Heavy-wall, flame-retardant, self-adhesive heat-shrink tubing. All-weather, all-size insulation for harsh environments, the catalog copy bragged. It sounded like overkill to me, but better safe than sorry. A watertight seal was all I really needed. Two-inch-diameter tubing came in six-inch lengths and shrank down to .60 inches in diameter. The inside diameter of a wine bottle neck is .70 inches. Wonders never cease. I smiled. Red or black? Black would be undetectable in the red wine in case it pressed against the inside of the bottle.

Next, DHL. I didn't usually schedule pickups at 1:00 in the morning, so it wasn't my service rep who answered the phone. Not used to providing any account numbers since they knew me on a first name basis, I had to put the phone down to shuffle through papers to find an old receipt. Nerve-wracking, Niki, I talked out loud to myself.

Next on the list: floor space for the hundred cases. I could move five cases at a time stacked on the hand truck. More than that was too wobbly and too heavy. Twenty stacks of cases would take up about 25 x 18 feet of space. If I pushed all the tables against the walls and put the chairs up, I'd have just enough space if I also used the hallway to the backroom. Every detail like this, that I hadn't considered, would add precious minutes and make the night that much longer. I reminded myself of all the nights Costa and I were up until dawn, working until two a.m., closing and cleaning, then going to the beach to unwind. I had no reason to worry about one more sleepless night, and called the LA wine storage to reserve a space. I was getting nervous that I might miss them, as it was late afternoon there. They would certainly take delivery even without a reservation, but why risk it? Even a mysterious shipment of wine would be whisked into a climate-controlled unit, handled with utmost care so as not to bruise the precious juice.

I headed over to Ugo's shop to start the order and pull the bottles. It was just 1:50 in the morning. It would take me at least an hour to pull all the bottles I needed. The shop seemed more cluttered and dusty than usual. Ugo had no touch when it came to maintaining the shop's appearance. I headed straight for the office computer in the backroom and pulled up an old order which I duplicated, and I upped the quantity to 100 cases. I left one copy on Ugo's desk and took another for myself. I pulled the bottles, filled the cases, and staged them at the front door: 3:00 a.m.

I retracted a bollard, one of the small cement obelisks spaced at intervals to keep cars off the sidewalk, and backed the Jeep right up to the door so I wouldn't have to maneuver the hand truck over the uneven step at the entrance. Thank goodness there weren't any steps to deal with at the wine bar. I could fit fourteen cases in the Jeep. It would take eight trips back and forth—just over two hours, I estimated. I kept the light on at the wine bar and from Ugo's shop could see it less than a block away. I didn't even bother to close the doors or turn off the engine at either end. The street was deserted, and I could shave some minutes off my time if I didn't lock up.

After thirty minutes of nonstop hauling, I took a breather. I could rest while I printed the mailing labels. I needed to find the database in the computer where the addresses were kept— one thing I hadn't done before. I typed *addresses* in the search box on the desktop. The computer hummed and clicked as it worked. Nothing. What nonsensical word had Ugo filed the addresses under? I decided it would be faster to scroll through folders hoping it would jump out at me. Finally, a folder labeled *Customers* looked promising. I double clicked and inside it were more folders: *poto, bar*; *kafe, café*; *zeno, hotel*; *esti, restaurant*—all abbreviated titles—and one called *posto*. Voila! I quickly scrolled through the spreadsheet, found a random Thai address, brought up the print box, typed 9 for page quantity and loaded the tray with mailing labels.

While the printer swallowed, then regurgitated the paper, I glanced at the other folders on the desktop. There were places and names, mostly Asian-sounding, some I'd heard Thof talk about, many I hadn't heard of before. Then I saw a folder named *Brielle*. What the...? My heart fluttered in my throat. I double clicked. Inside was an untitled document and another folder titled *foto*.

I quickly toggled through the untitled images: Thof and Brielle arm in arm, holding a business license in front of them; Thof and Brielle shaking hands in front of Ugo's shop; Brielle shaking Ugo's hand; Thof, Brielle, and Ugo holding a magnum bottle of champagne together, showing off Ugo's label; Thof, Brielle, and Ugo cutting a cluster of grapes in the vineyard. Hold on. It can't be. The three of them were business partners? I couldn't believe my eyes. How much did Ugo know about Brielle's past—or present, for that matter? My stomach gripped tightly as I considered all the possibilities. I had to get back to moving the cases. I wanted to be finished before sunrise and there were still six trips to make, but that untitled document was staring me in the face.

Chop-chop, Niki! I'll give you sixty seconds. I double clicked. The computer was fantastically slow, moaning and clacking like an old woman. The entire screen flickered, then the page opened. Six lines, three columns—bank names, account numbers, and dollar amounts: Grand Caymen Trust, $2.4; Carib First, $4.1; Euro Pacific Bank, $5.6; Caye Bank Belize, $8.5; HSBC Hong Kong, $12.2. So Ugo had been involved in Thof's dealings all along! The idea suddenly put the fear of God in me. Images of my encounters with Thof's father boiled up in my mind—when I ran off to Turkey with Costa and left the wine bar repair to him, when he told me he had never balanced the books, the time he delivered the envelope with my divorce papers. I sensed he had looked at them. Oh, Niki, ignorance was bliss. Once again, I broke out into a sweat and forced myself to shut the computer down. The added adrenaline made me move even faster.

At 5:30 a.m. I loaded the last of the cases, turned the lights off at Ugo's, and locked the door. Rivulets of sweat rolled down my back even in the coolness of the morning. I wanted just a minute off my feet, but there was no place to sit in the wine bar with all the chairs up on the tables and the floor completely occupied with boxes. I lifted the front of my shirt to wipe the sweat from my forehead and it dawned on me that I'd forgotten the heat gun from Ugo's. Damn it, you should have double-checked the list. I turned on my heels to run back down the street when I saw a silhouette of a large man standing in the still open door of the bar.

"Aaaaaah!" I screamed. "Jesus! Nasir, you scared the shit out of me! How long have you been standing there? Why are you sneaking around?" My hand reflexively went to my mouth, covering it, cringing for cursing and embarrassed that he'd seen my exposed chest.

"The door was open. Delivering napkins." He stood stock-still. Two bundles of bleached, pressed napkins were cradled in his arms like a baby. I'd completely forgotten about his early morning deliveries. There had been times, walking back from the beach at dawn when I'd seen his bundles sitting outside the doorways of cafes and hotels—sheets, towels, tablecloths.

Entrance lights shined down on them in the darkness of morning, like a ray of sunlight. I'd never seen him, just the white bundles, tidy packages tied with string.

"Busy," he said.

Was it a question or a statement?

"Uh, yes, getting a jump on the day. Big shipment going out. Giving Ugo a hand since Thof is gone," I said, still shocked and embarrassed.

He nodded and retreated out the door as silently as he'd entered.

"Thanks," I called after him weakly.

Thank gawd he headed down the street in the opposite direction of Ugo's. I jogged the distance, unlocked the door again, found the heat gun, and headed back. How much of my locking and unlocking had he seen? Did it matter, I wondered as I madly started labeling the cases, peeling the fake shipping labels off the printer paper and slapping them on the boxes as I made my way up and down the stacked aisles. I glanced at my watch. 6:00 a.m. Right on schedule.

20

Back at the apartment I made coffee and reviewed my list in the dark quiet. I missed Minky's soft meows and brushes against my legs asking for her breakfast. Costa would be waking up soon at Selena's. The sound of a plane engine throttling, heading out over the sea, made me fantasize about being up there, safe, heading home.

The shower pounded luxuriously against the aches that had set into my back and arms. I set the alarm for 8:00 a.m. and finished my coffee. Drinking coffee throughout the day kept a buzz going, but if I was extremely tired, like now, it put me to sleep. I would often have a cup before a nap and wake up refreshed. Just to be safe, I set both alarms, one on each side of the bed. As I dozed off, I remembered again that I hadn't returned the bank manager's call. I subconsciously had never intended on calling him back. I couldn't face whatever it was that he needed to tell me. What a crazy risk I was willing to take in order to avoid him.

I woke up to both alarms going off at once and for a moment thought it was funny that we'd both set our alarms for exactly the same time. But where was Thof? Reality percolated slowly into my brain, like the caffeine I'd drunk a few hours earlier. It felt like days had gone by, not just a few hours. Shit. This is real, I thought, and kicked into gear. I threw on a sweatshirt and jeans but changed my mind, putting more thought into how I looked. Presentation is everything, I always said—my former life as a graphic designer coming back to me. When I requested the cash at the bank last week, I'd been flirting unabashedly with the manager. I'd best pick up where I left off but with a bit more flare—or dare, should I say? I chose the same cardigan, but this time put a little push-up bra under it and unbuttoned it down to semi-scandalous. Instead of the blue dress, I decided on a flippy cheerleader-like skirt. My rule was: tight on the top, loose on the bottom, or vice versa. Never tight on both top and bottom! I added the hat and scarf again to cover the fading bruises on my head and neck, along with sunglasses, red lipstick, and now that I was steadier on my feet, high heels. That should keep the manager amply distracted.

I grabbed two canvas shopping bags and hopped into the Jeep. It was a short mile to the bank, but I didn't want to walk the cobbled streets in high heels—or carry twenty pounds' worth of cash all the way back home. The bank parking lot was empty except for the employees' cars. Was this the right way to do it—arriving at opening time when there would be no other customers? No distractions? I tried to convince myself that no matter how much thought I put into it, there was no way to know how the transaction would go down. Breathe, Niki, in through the nose, out through the mouth. Big belly breath. Again. Teeth check. Smile now, a big honeymoon smile. Lookin' good.

I forced myself to walk slowly, casually. It gave me time to scan the bank tellers. Where was my guy?

"Hello! How may I help you today?" a chirpy young woman shouted out from behind her window before I was even halfway across the small lobby.

"I'm here to see Sami," I smiled, covering my irritation at her perkiness.

"He's in a meeting right now. He'll be out shortly. May I

help you with anything?" Again, the trained customer service, false cheer, and squeaky child voice.

I reflexively lowered my pitch. "I'll wait, thanks."

"Help yourself to tea or coffee, please," she gestured to a wobbly tray on fold-out legs at the other end of the room.

I gave her a vacuous smile and headed toward the beverages. I thumbed through the tea choices, pondering them as though choosing the correct one would determine the outcome of the meeting. Better make it herbal; I didn't need any caffeine jitters or the bad breath it always seemed to stir up. I was starting to lose my Zen mind, getting more antsy by the second. I sipped the tea too soon and scorched my tongue. Shit! I put the full cup back down on the tray.

"Niki." His voice, low and slow, was suddenly at my back. I twirled around and nearly fell into his outstretched hand.

"Sami, good to see you." I licked my lips, feeling my singed tongue, and took his hand.

"I wasn't sure when you were coming. Did you get my message?" His hair was tousled just like the first time I'd met him. "Please, follow me."

"I'm so sorry. I was visiting a friend out of town—long-distance call and all. I didn't want to bother her with it." I trailed after him into a private room.

"Well, no problem at all." He seemed so casual as he closed the door behind him, with none of the official business manner he had the last time. "Have a seat."

"Was there a problem?" Please no! I screamed in my head.

"Not at all, not at all. It was… uh… well, a personal matter." He avoided my eyes as he opened a cabinet in the wall and removed a tray of cash banded in equal stacks.

"Oh?" I stared as he turned back toward me—Greek men with their black hair and searing blue eyes.

"I was going to suggest you come at a time when you could join me for lunch or a drink. But it's a little early for that now, I suppose." His teeth were perfect. "I'm glad that you brought some bags. I was going to suggest that too—something inconspicuous. Perfect."

I tried not to stare at the money. Luckily, he was quite a distraction. My gawd, Niki, does it ever end? I almost had to laugh at myself—teetering on the edge of a knife, manipulating this situation, all the while thinking about what I'd like to do with this boy-man. Now I was getting hot. I took my sweater off and put it in one of the bags on top of the money.

"Coffee perhaps?" he proposed as he took the bags from me and packed them with no more fanfare than if he were bagging my groceries.

"Oh no, thanks. I had some of your tea," I said.

"Well, at a café, I meant." He finally looked up, handing the bags back to me, indicating we were finished here.

"Oh! That's so nice of you to offer and I greatly appreciate all the trouble you've gone through for me. It's just that I'm leaving in a few days… you know… to meet Thof, and I have some other appointments that I'm on my way to right now. I could maybe squeeze it in tomorrow afternoon?" Just when I'm boarding a plane, I thought.

"*Téleios*," he purred. *Perfect.* "Four o'clock? Café Xenon?"

"See you then." I gave him my brightest come-on smile and hightailed it out of there and headed across the parking lot toward the Jeep.

"Niki!" I heard shouting from the front door of the bank. I kept walking because that voice with its particular twang was not the bank manager's. I didn't have time for interruptions now.

"Niki girl!" Chuck came trotting up.

Damn damn damn. There was no escaping now. I turned to say hello, but kept walking at a fast clip.

"Let me help you with those bags. They look heavy. Did you just rob the bank?" He burst out laughing and bounced up and down on his toes as he grabbed the bag that had my sweater on top.

"Hey, Chuck. Sorry, I'm really in a hurry. Gotta get to work. Just picking up some donations for the canned food drive we're having at Koraki. Canned beans. Yup. Pretty heavy, but I can manage. See you tonight?"

"Suit yourself, missy. Save me a seat!" He hoisted the bag into the Jeep.

"Bye!" I waved and cursed silently.

...

Adrenalin masked the exhaustion now, and light-headedness made me giddy. I pushed the bags onto the floor of the Jeep and headed home. I took the stairs two at time with one bag over each shoulder. A box from the hardware store was at the front door—the shrink-wrap tubes. I made a mental note to check that off the list, kicked the box through the door, dumped the bags on the living room floor, and ripped off my clothes, replacing them with a pair of old jeans, a sports bra, and a sweatshirt. What a fucking relief! I did a back flop onto the bed, arms and legs splayed like a starfish, stared at the ceiling, and allowed myself to laugh out loud. Now where's that list?

"Stay calm" was the first thing on today's list. I think I was off to a good start on that item. Bank: check; hardware delivery: check; hydrate. I needed to add that to the list, and I chugged a glass of water. What next? If push came to shove, I could head to the airport without packing a single thing. I needed to start practicing on some bottles and forgo packing. That would be a luxury if I had the time in the end. Prudence.

I broke open the delivery box to find funny noodle-y, tube thingies, just as they were pictured in the catalog. They smelled like rubber tires. That could pose a problem. Would I need ventilation? I unearthed a small fan from the closet, grabbed a few wine bottles from the kitchen shelf, the heat gun, foils, a corkscrew, and a stack of cash, which I realized I hadn't even bothered to look at yet. It wasn't that impressive. Not like in the movies. But I reminded myself these were hundred-dollar bills, not ones. It was starting to sink in.

I uncorked the first bottle and poured out less than half a cup, I guessed. The additional weight of about twenty pounds worth of cash divided among 100 cases would be a wash with the four ounces or so I'd have to empty from the bottles; DHL and customs would not be alerted. I plugged in the heat gun, grabbed a bundle of cash and a noodle-y tube, slipped the paper band off the stack and roughly divided it in half, then compared the two stacks and evened them out a little more. I wasn't about to count exactly half—fifty notes—out of every stack. Half a bundle was less than a quarter of an inch thick. I'd have to do this 200 times to get through it all. Jesus.

I rolled the bills lengthwise and fed them into a tube, allowing about a half inch of extra length on each end—easy enough. I turned on the heat gun. It was hot after just a few seconds, and I aimed it at the tube. Miraculously, it shriveled and tightened around the money, squeezing it into a seamless, snug package, like a shiny condom. This was easier than rolling a joint—took about ten seconds and no smell! I pushed the compressed tube into the neck of a bottle—a tight fit, but it made it in—and poured out a little more wine so it would level right above the foil. I pounded the cork back in and slipped a foil over the neck, hit it with the heat gun, and instantly, the foil sucked up tight against the bottle. I couldn't believe how fast and easy the whole process was. I could make all my cash rolls this morning in the apartment and have them ready to go for tonight. One huge step ahead of schedule.

It was noon now. I got my assembly line going—cutting a handful of tubes at a time to the length I needed and unpacking the cash out of the bag, but I felt nervous right away. What if someone came to the door or peeked through the deck window? The postman or Ugo? Who knew? I couldn't have all this money laid out on the living room floor, so I packed it back into the bags and moved to the bedroom floor.

I laid out the flimsy tubes and cash again and plugged in the heat gun behind the bedside table. The job went fast, but every time I burned myself with the heat gun I cursed and reminded myself to be more careful. I divided the cash-filled tubes between the two bags. It was easier carrying a bag in both hands than being weighed down by one heavy bag, and even though they were compressed down to less than half their original volume, they still weighed twenty pounds. Don't muscle through this, Niki. Pace yourself. I threw the heat gun and foils in the bag, too, and drove to the wine bar. I wanted the Jeep close by in case anything happened and I needed a quick escape.

What was I going to do all day? I wouldn't be able to concentrate on anything, but I had to make it look like I was working, even though the bar was closed now, like all the businesses were, for a short break before the winter holidays. Normally, like everyone else, I'd be doing inventory, cleaning, planning—all the chores to be ready for the new year, but none of that mattered now. As I pulled up to the wine bar, I noticed the door was ajar. The only people with keys were Costa and Ugo, and I knew Costa wasn't back yet. I shoved the bags of money underneath the seats. Thank gawd I'd kept them in two bags. They were completely out of sight.

"Ugo?" I called out before I was through the door.

"Niki! I came in early when I got your message that a large shipment needed to go out and what a surprise I found—even larger than what you said it would be."

It was the most words I'd ever heard him speak at one time and with such enthusiasm. "All that was left to do was tape the boxes shut," he added.

"You taped the boxes shut? I wasn't finished with the paperwork." I tried to calm down. How much would I have to undo?

"Yes, and I called DHL. They said they weren't scheduled to pick up until tomorrow. How silly. I changed it to this afternoon."

"Oh! No. I mean… Thof just called and made some changes. That's why I scheduled it for tomorrow. I was expecting last-minute changes from him." Holy crap. Recover, Niki!

"Why does he not call me?" Ugo asked.

"He doesn't want to wake you at odd hours. I don't mind. I want to talk to him anyway, of course. I miss him. That's why I did all this work last night. I couldn't sleep, thinking about him. Please, no worries. I'll make the changes and call DHL. I need something to do." I tried not to sound like I was pleading. What had gotten into him? In an entire year, I'd never seen him so lucid and chatty.

"*Sígouros, entáxei,*" he mumbled—*Sure, okay*—back to his old self with his two-word sentences, and he walked out the door without saying anything else.

Shit. Am I going to have a heart attack? What's next? I raced to the phone and rescheduled DHL back to tomorrow morning, then set into the cases with my box cutter, opening all that he'd taped shut—luckily, not many, since the place was so jammed. You could hardly move between the stacks. I'm going to have to shuffle each one to get inside all the boxes. It's like a sliding puzzle. There's no place to go with it all!

That's a hell of a lot of lifting again for one night. I felt my body slump at the thought of it. My stomach simultaneously let out a loud growl. Oh, yes, hello. Did someone forget about you?

It felt like days since I'd eaten. Or was it hours? The days and nights were melding into one long dream-like state.

21

I made a quick run to the deli around the corner. The line was longer than I'd ever seen it, since it was the only place nearby that was open. I forced myself to join in the small talk the other customers made—local business owners all doing the same year-end chores that I was supposedly doing—but I was tapping my foot and starting to huff when it occurred to me that I'd better calm down before I went ballistic. What did I have to do all afternoon but kill time and ruminate? Twenty-five minutes ticked by like an eternity. Finally, I paid for my souvlaki and hoofed it back to the bar. The warmth of the pita bread in my hand and the smell of the lamb, with its dripping juices made my mouth water. I couldn't believe how hungry I was. I peeled the paper back from the souvlaki, took a bite, and walked as fast as I could without calling attention to myself. The meat juices mingled with the mint-spiked tzatziki and a pale greenish trail of it ran down my arm. Oh, heaven. My stomach thanked me. I nodded, mouth full, to my neighbors carrying their own lunches back to their shuttered businesses.

Looking toward the wine bar I stopped dead in my tracks. Where was the Jeep? No! No! No! I'd completely forgotten I left the money under the seats when I got sidetracked by Ugo. This has got to be a joke, a bad dream. This cannot be happening!

I broke into a run, my souvlaki losing its contents. A note was taped to the door of the wine bar, addressed to Thof. Where did I recognize that handwriting from? Holding a corner of the envelope with my souvlaki hand, I ripped it open with my other hand, smearing it with grease.

> What happened to you? Where are you?
> Where's my money?
> —B

The money! My stomach clamped down like my clenched fist around my souvlaki, the greasy, lamby smell lingering in my nose. I unlocked the door to the wine bar and stumbled in, slammed the door shut behind me, and threw the mangled souvlaki into the trash. Think, think, Niki. Costa had spare keys to the Jeep. Maybe he'd gotten home from Selena's and come by for it. But that means he most likely ran into Brielle. I had been gone for twenty-five minutes. I supposed that was plenty of time for both to come and go without seeing each other, except Costa had to have arrived first. He would have taken the note off the door if it was there when he arrived. If they did run into each other, would he think to cover for me or did Brielle go to Ugo's?

Fictional thinking, Niki! No one knows I have the money, not even Costa. There's nothing for him to spill except that Thof was in jail. Brielle doesn't know me, so why would she have any suspicions of me with the money? I was getting carried away now, a little paranoid. I needed to carry on. Costa knows Brielle is a snake. He knows I'm leaving tomorrow. Would he keep her distracted? I looked at my watch. Three o'clock. I had to get the money back from the Jeep. That was the priority, regardless of Brielle. I locked up again and made the twenty-minute walk to Costa's apartment.

There it was, parked right outside his door. I grabbed the bags from their hiding place under the seats and turned to head back when I heard his apartment door open. I prayed to be invisible and didn't dare turn around. I just kept walking, head down.

"Niki! Niki! Wait!" It was Selena shouting in the street as I rounded the corner. White-knuckling my bags, I stopped and peeked around the corner.

"Selena!" I whispered. "What are you doing here?" Why was I whispering?

"Niki, thank God." She put her hand on my back and gently urged me forward. "Keep walking." Now she was whispering too. "Costa and I got here forty-five minutes ago. I had a strong feeling that something was wrong. Last night I made an excuse to come to town today."

Selena looked up, then down the street.

"Are you okay?" she asked me. We kept walking toward the wine bar. "That woman is evil."

"So you ran into Brielle? Where is she? Where's Costa?" I was about to crack.

"When we didn't find you at your apartment, Costa and I stopped by the wine bar. We waited, but when you didn't come back, we took the Jeep and headed back to Costa's. He assured me you were probably nearby running errands, and you'd call him if you needed it. We stopped for a cup of coffee along the way and that's when we ran into *her*." She spit the word out as though it was poison on her tongue. "I told Costa I wanted to get my car so I could do my errands— that I didn't want to wait for the two of them to catch up, so he invited her to ride with us. When he dropped me at my car in front of his apartment, I was able to tell him to keep her occupied for as long as he could, and I gave him the stink eye." She screwed up her face, subtly raising her left eyebrow while narrowing her right eye. "He knows I'm serious when I do that. So they're at his place now and I was running out to find you when I saw you at the Jeep!" She was breathless relaying the story to me.

"But how did you know… I mean… what do you know?" I hesitated to ask.

"Poppet, I know you are up to something. Something I probably would not approve of, but I also know you're very close to danger and I'm here to help."

I stopped in my tracks, exposed in the middle of town. I was supposed to be lying low in the wine bar, not standing in the middle of the street, holding a half million dollars of cash in weird-looking tubes, where any banker, baker, or drug dealer could spot me.

"Let's get back to the wine bar," I whispered and took off ahead of her. When I looked over my shoulder to make sure she was keeping up, she was stopped on the sidewalk, talking to three old ladies. They turned in unison to look at me, the same crones that ran Pema and me out of their souvenir store when we insisted on getting our passports back. Every few yards someone else stopped Selena to say hello. I kept on going. She'd find out soon enough what my rush was about.

Fifteen minutes later she walked into the wine bar. The lights were low; she was just a silhouette.

"I'm in the back," I called out to her.

"Niki, what's going on? I can hardly even make it back there with all these cases."

"I don't want to drag you into this," I told her, trying to hold the tears back. Why tears now, Niki? Pull yourself together. "I'm sorry. I'm in over my head, I—"

"Niki, tell me what's going on. I'll help you, whatever it is. This is the shipment you helped Ugo with? It's way bigger than you said it would be. It's not real, is it?"

I told her everything then—about the photos I found of Brielle with Thof and Ugo, the money I took from Thof's wallet, Thof's method of stashing drugs in bottles, and the necessity of having to divert Ugo this morning, which was why I'd left the money in the Jeep.

"Oh, winter's ghost! You've certainly planned this out! What were you thinking when you took that check from Thof's wallet?"

"I wasn't thinking at all! I was beat up, in shock, and my

body took over. It was a reflex—methodical and precise, now that I think about it. I replaced everything in his wallet exactly as I'd found it, folded his clothes back up, and walked out. By the time I got back to Nafplio, it was settled in my mind what I was going to do."

I waited for her to lower the ax, to tell me to take the money back to the bank, and go to the police.

"Poppet, this is so dangerous. The consequences you could face from not only Brielle but from the law are insane. I don't know which would be worse."

"I'm so sorry. I should not have dragged you into this," I said. But now what? I thought. I'm in it up to my neck.

"We better get a move on," she said with a wry smile. "It's five o'clock; you have plenty of time. I'll guard the door, chase away any visitors, and get you fed. You're looking gaunt. I'll leave the heavy lifting to you."

"Oh my gawd. Seriously? Thank you." I laughed and cried at the same time with relief. "I owe you so much. In fact, take a tube," I grabbed a black rubbery money tube out of my bag and handed it to her.

"There's something about it that I don't want to touch." Selena stared at the tube, but didn't take it. "But I may need a little vacation to California someday."

"You got it!"

She sat on a case near the window, out of sight of passersby, and kept an eye out. I got started on the daunting task of un-corking. I replaced the altered bottles into the same two center positions in every box so I'd know which bottles they were once I got back to the States. I re-addressed the cases with California shipping labels, taping them shut as I went, me-thodically working my way from the back corner of the room to the front. This was the final push, the long haul. Selena's company kept me sane. I paced myself and took breaks and she made coffee and brought us food to last through the night.

"How will you get to the airport?" Selena asked as I worked. "Should I schedule a taxi?"

"I was going to take the Jeep. I hadn't planned on Costa being back in town, much less Brielle! I was going to park it at the airport and mail his keys back to him."

"Well, you can't do that now—not with her here. Take my car. It'll be one less thing for Costa to be questioned about—his missing car. She doesn't know mine and no one else will recognize it either. In fact, I'll go get it now. Drop the keys in a mailbox like you had planned as soon as you get to the airport. I'll have them back in a day. There's plenty I can do in town and that way I can keep track of her—send her off on a wild goose chase if I can."

"You don't think Costa has told her that Thof is in jail?"

"Oh, no. He got my message loud and clear. She'll learn nothing from him."

"Let's hope so. As I recall, the last time they were together he had quite the hangover."

...

Once it was dark, it was reasonably safe to assume that no one would drop in. Selena left her post at the window to walk back to Costa's and pick up her car, re-parking it around the corner from the wine bar. The night passed with no surprises, but maneuvering the cases proved to be problematic in the tight space and slowed things down. DHL was scheduled to arrive at eight a.m., but by six I knew I wouldn't make it. Selena called to delay them, but was told they were already en route and would arrive as scheduled.

"Shit, shit, shit." My center rose for the first time again after such a calm night. "Selena, will you help? You can foil the bottles as I hand them to you, and quick, label the rest of the boxes." I doubled my pace.

DHL arrived right on time at eight a.m. There were still twenty boxes to do.

"Hi, guys. I'm still working on this, but you can start loading. Will take you a while," I told the driver.

"I brought a helper," he said. "Didn't want to get behind schedule on the rest of my day. So this shouldn't take long at all, miss," the driver said.

I didn't care if they saw what I was doing. They would have no clue. Anyway, their heads were down schlepping boxes. We cranked out the bottles as fast as we could go. There were only eight boxes left when they finished loading.

"Selena, will you take them outside to finish the paperwork?" I asked her. *Slowly!* I mouthed.

"I'll be right outside to sign your papers in just a minute," I heard her tell them. "I have to go to the ladies room first."

Oh, Selena, you are a gem, I thought. The driver rolled his eyes with impatience, lit up a cigarette, and paced on the sidewalk. Selena finally emerged from the bathroom as I sealed the last box.

The bar was empty, my body was frazzled, and I felt dizzy at the thought of the money being released into the hands of others to complete the journey. Hell, even if something happened to it, I didn't care. I was glad for it to be out of there, but now my window of time to catch an early flight out was closing. If I missed the last morning flight I'd have to wait until evening, or else fly to Rome, the closest connection with the most flights back to the States. I'd go anywhere to get out of Greece and away from Brielle and Ugo bearing down on me. I stood in the wine bar's doorway and took one last look.

"We did it," I said to Selena.

"You did it. Good riddance to that! But no time for sentiment or for packing a bag, either. Get going. We'll be in touch." Selena gave me a quick hug and the keys to the car.

"Oh, I almost forgot. I saved a little something for the trip." I winked at her and headed behind the bar to grab a laundered bottle I'd stashed on the bottom shelf, just in case I needed some extra cash on my trip, not to mention a swig of good wine.

"Excuse me, I'm looking for Niki," a woman's voice spoke in Greek. I almost dropped the bottle. I held my breath and clutched the bottle to my chest as if it would protect me. I didn't dare make a move and stayed frozen down on my knees behind the bar.

"Hello, Brielle," Selena managed. I heard her shuffling a pile of mail on the bar. "Where's Costa?"

"I'm looking for Niki," Brielle repeated, ignoring Selena's question.

"Niki left last week to meet Thof and a big shipment in Thailand. I'm giving Costa a hand until they get back. Is Costa with you?" She spoke in a grandmotherly tone, not reacting to Brielle's brusqueness.

"Costa is sleeping it off. Do you have an address?"

"Of course. Here's the shipping order. Take it," Selena said, handing her Ugo's old paperwork.

Brielle left without saying a word.

"Holy shit!" I whispered to Selena, "That was her! She's on to me." A trembling started in my stomach. Muscle spasms traveled up my spine to my head. I couldn't control the shaking, as though I was shivering in the cold.

"Niki, *calmé, calmé*. She's gone now, to the opposite end of the world. You have nothing to worry about except getting yourself to the airport."

I gave Selena the quickest hug and ran to the car, parked two spaces in from the corner. No one was in front of it, making for a fast getaway.

22

The traffic was very light at 8:30 in the morning. I got to the airport in record time. There was a flight to Amsterdam in an hour. There would be plenty of flights to LA from there. I had time to buy an envelope and stamp to mail Selena's keys back to her and grab a bite to eat. I realized I was still holding my breath—taking in big gulps of air, then holding it in my chest. I had to calm down. It was all done now; nothing at all left for me to do. As exhausted as I was, I kept walking, browsing through the magazine and book stands to keep myself distracted. An hour felt like forever, but finally they called for boarding.

Passengers pressed forward through the gangway, pushing their luggage along ploddingly slow. The line stopped at the door to the airplane, waiting for someone in first class to get themselves settled into their seat. I dreaded the wait, giving me time to inspect the bolts on the outside of the plane that held the metal panels together. Were they all tightened down? Would they peel off the plane in midair? And the tiny gap between the gangway and the plane where I could see down to the tarmac below made my stomach drop thinking about having to step over it. What the hell was taking so long? Come on, let's get this show on the road! Finally I stepped into the plane.

"Stewardess, I'd like a drink now. And an eye mask too," the woman who had been holding up the line groused before she was even seated.

Greek. Female. Rude. No. *No no no no no*! My mind was tricking me; my body moved into fight, flight, or freeze mode.

There she was, the woman in the photos, the voice in the wine bar this morning, standing by the curtain separating first-class from cattle-class. Passengers shoved past her. She was dressed in skyscraper-high heels made of snake skin with red soles—the only adornment in an otherwise boardroom-looking outfit: A-line skirt, tailored silk shirt, sunglasses, and dark red lipstick. Even behind the sunglasses I could sense her glaring, seething expression. She was like a viper, long and slithering. The stewardess was clearly out of her comfort zone and fumbled to oblige.

"I do not want a window seat," Brielle bitched again to the stewardess.

"I'm sorry ma'am… uh… miss? It was the very last seat. Normally there are no seats available at the last minute."

Brielle huffed and fell into her seat as though all at once the air was knocked out of her.

I snapped back to my senses, realizing I was in full view of her. I took my hat off my head and shielded my face with it. My scarf still covered my hair. What was I doing? So obviously hiding my face. I was trapped and exposed, literally three feet from her. She has never seen you! I reminded myself and finally the line moved again and I joined everyone else, this time in pressing into the person in front of me in an attempt to push them forward. Move!

I found my seat. The weight lifting off my chest was palpable, the adrenaline slowly dissipating, like icicles melting drop by drop—which gradually turned into tears. It was as though my body was ahead of my mind. I didn't feel the emotions of crying, yet tears streamed down my face. The passengers filed into the plane. I read their faces and made up stories about what they did and who they might be. I caught myself sighing out loud. My brain was telling me to relax, but I couldn't help but be jittery. I flipped through the airline magazine distractedly and continued analyzing the faces of the boarding passengers. I rifled through the seat pocket again, looking for I don't know what. In my thoughts I went back to the apartment and wondered if there was anything of importance I'd left behind. Nothing. I sunk further down into my seat and put the magazine up in front of my face, too scared to look. Too scared to be seen.

It was going to be a three-hour-and-forty-five-minute flight of torture to Amsterdam. No amount of Bloody Marys could calm me down now. I talked myself through a new rush of adrenaline. We would part ways at the gate. She would be heading east, and I was heading west. She'd take an underground tram to the Asia terminal, and I would take a surface bus to the U.S. terminal. Sounds right. She'll deplane first; I'll hang back. Or should I shove forward so I can keep an eye on her? Oh my gawd, what should I do? Relax. That's what you should do. You have almost four hours to decide. She won't leave her first-class compartment. Just get a drink! I resisted the urge to steal a bottle from the unattended galley or better yet, open my own. I stayed hunkered down in my seat, covered with a blanket and buried in the airline magazine. I wasn't able to read a single word, and just sat looking at pictures of oversized cardboard cat houses and Gifts for What Every Man Dreams Of! with no eye contact with anyone. I made myself as small and invisible as possible as the stewardess labored through her seat buckle air mask flotation device children elderly smoking customs routine. Cartons of cigarettes were available! Yay! How about a quart of Bloody Marys!

I kept reminding myself I had nothing to worry about; Brielle had never seen me. We had crossed each other's paths so many times but never met: the day she left the note with pills in it for Thof, the night I spent alone in the Bosphorus while she and Thof had dinner together, two days ago when she left another note for Thof asking where her money was and was intercepted by Costa and Selena, and finally this morning at the wine bar. That's a hell of a lot of near misses! As far as she was concerned, I didn't even exist; that is, until this morning. At least I was certain that Costa hadn't told her anything; otherwise she would not have taken the bait from Selena that Thof and I were in Thailand.

Finally the plane lifted off, and the second-class cart made its way through the cabin as the nervous, first-class stewardess flitted back and forth with glasses of champagne, and who knows what else, to the other side of the curtain.

"Miss? Beverage?" the stewardess asked me.

"Two Bloody Marys, please," I whispered. "I'll pay extra."

"Excuse me, miss; you'll have to speak up." The perky stewardess may as well have shouted through a megaphone. I slunk down even further and gave her a helpless look. The man sitting beside me looked down at me, then up at the stewardess, rolled his eyes at her, and relayed my request.

"No problem, miss." She handed me two cans of V8 tomato juice and two mini-bottles of vodka with a pitying look.

"I used to be scared of flying, too," the man said, winking at me. "You can hold my hand if you want. Here, take my water, too. Trust me, you'll feel like shit tomorrow if you don't." He put his cup of water on my tray and his hand on top of mine. This time I was the one rolling my eyes. Could this get any weirder?

By the time we landed I was so stiff from hunching down in my seat and so sluggish from the drinks that I used the seat in front of me to hoist myself up. When they opened the divider curtain, I was hidden in the crowd of impatient passengers unloading the overhead bins, keeping an eye on the first-class snake to make sure she and her fancy shoes exited with the rest of first class. I hung back, letting other passengers pass to give the bitch plenty of time to put some distance between us, but eventually I had to get off the plane. I picked up my handbag, the weight of the wine bottle in it giving me comfort. I tentatively made my way down the aisle and into the gangway, where I found myself hugging the wall as passengers pushed past, huffing and glaring at me for holding them up. I stopped at the entrance to the terminal to scan the crowd one last time when a man slammed into my back.

"Geez! We're on the ground now. Could you keep it moving?" he gruffed. It was the man I'd been sitting beside, rebuffed when I didn't hold his hand.

"Geez yourself," I said without thinking and stepped around the corner into the light of the terminal to let him pass. I hugged my bag tight against my chest and sighed deeply. What's the worst-case scenario? I asked myself. What could she do to me in the middle of a crowded airport? Take me hostage? Shoot me with a poison dart? Geez myself! I had a connection to Los Angeles and my future to catch!

23

First class was all I'd hoped it would be—champagne, smiles, slippers, and space! I'd upgraded as soon as I found my gate. What the hell; I should get used to it. The champagne knocked me out before we even took off. I woke up refreshed, though disoriented, with a moment of not knowing where I was or where I was going, then was stunned when the stewardess told me only three hours to landing. I'd slept for eight hours! A smile spread across my face. When was the last time that happened? My mind was free to drift in this flying cloak of safety. I remembered the bank manager and wondered how long he'd waited for me at the cafe. And where did Brielle think she was going to find us in Thailand? She'd find out when she got there that she'd been given a bogus address. I supposed she and Thof had other meeting spots there. Hotels, no doubt. There was so much I'd never know.

I remembered Pema's letter in my bag—it was one of the few items I'd grabbed before leaving—that and the fox charm Thof had given me when we first met. I dug them both out of my bag and reread the letter. It had been in the back of my mind since I received it months ago. I'd probably been processing it subconsciously since then, because I knew exactly what I wanted to tell her. Pema had decided to keep the baby and she hoped that I would meet her someday. A rush of emotion welled up in me. In veering wildly off the course of my life that crazy summer two years ago, I changed others' lives too: my ex-husband's to start with, Pema's, and Thof's. They weren't all bad endings, though. Selena will be a cherished friend for life, as will Costa, no matter who he ends up with. And now there will be Pema and her baby. My eyes teared up in gratitude and I wrote the letter to Pema that she'd been waiting for for way too long.

> Dear Pema,
>
> I'm so happy to hear the news of your baby
> girl and am honored that you want me to
> meet her. I'm sorry it's taken me so long to
> respond. A lot has happened, but we can
> catch up on that later. In the meantime, I'm
> literally flying back to the States as I write this
> letter, excited to start (another) new life. I'll be
> at the Zen retreat center near Stinson Beach
> for a few weeks, then plan on finding a little
> place by the beach in Laguna. I'll call you
> with the details as soon as I'm settled.
> Will you fly out, baby on board, to see me?!
>
> I can't wait to meet the little one and see you
> again.
>
> Love, Niki
>
> PS: I'm setting up a trust for her (will explain
> later). She'll have no financial worries.

I folded the letter and put it back in my bag to mail once we landed, and rolled the fox charm between my fingers like a talisman, warm and smooth. As it heated up in my hand, I remembered the good times Thof and I had, and the things he opened up in me that no one else could ever have done—the dark creative powers of energy, ecstasy, and the ancient wisdom of the pack. My pack. Our pack.

"Ahem."

I was immersed in thought when the presence of the man sitting across the aisle from me entered into my consciousness. I looked up from my pensive introspection to find I was being stared at by an exotically handsome man with the blackest eyes of an old soul, and by the look of his biceps, very well built.

"I'm sorry to bother you… you seem very deep in thought," he said.

"Uh, yes, I suppose I am… was," I said.

"I'm Kitsune." He offered his hand across the aisle. "Kitsune Fox."

"Aah!" I jumped in my seat as my hand reflexively clenched the fox charm and stabbed my palm. "Fox? As in the animal?" I asked him.

"That's right," he said. "Double fox, in fact. Kitsune means fox in Japanese."

"You've got to be kidding me."

"Why?" he asked with a wry smile.

I opened my hand and showed him my fox lying in a pinprick of blood in my palm.

"Poor thing," he said, pushing the fox aside and touching the blood with his fingertip.

"Me or him?" I asked.

"Him," he answered, pointing to the fox. "I'm not worried about you." He looked up at me then as he put his finger in his mouth, tasting my blood, and quietly mimicked the yipping of a fox.

I stared at him incredulously. His eyes held mine like a raft holds a body floating on a deep blue lagoon.

"Where are you headed?" I finally broke through the spell he had on me.

"The San Francisco Dharma center. It's near Stinson Beach, in the redwoods. I'm a spiritual guide," he said, still holding my palm.

ABOUT THE AUTHOR

Gini Chin is a graphic designer, artist and writer who lives in Portland, Oregon, with her rescue dog, Minnow.
She has a BA from the University of Oregon with a minor in French and a major in graphic design. She owned a wine bar in a small coastal town in Washington. Previously, she enucleated eyes (removed them from donors) for the eye bank in Portland, Oregon.

www.ginichin.com